PERMANENT EMOTION

PERMANENT
EMOTION

Stories from the
Northern Short Story
Festival Academy

edited by
SJ Bradley

Valley Press

First published in 2024 by Valley Press
Woodend, The Crescent, Scarborough, UK, YO11 2PW
www.valleypressuk.com

ISBN 978-1-915606-44-0
Cat. no. VP0231

Cover and text design by Jamie McGarry.

Printed and bound in Great Britain by
Imprint Digital, Upton Pyne, Exeter.

Contents

Content Warnings

Baby loss
'Woven Together in the Depths of the Earth'

Graphic descriptions of violence, child peril
'Ototicular Dust', 'Food Chain'

Grief and loss; chronic illness and trauma
'Duckie', 'Silent Cure', 'Gabriel's Rocket', 'You Win'

Acknowledgements

This book, and the Academy scheme itself, only exists due to the support of the following organisations and funders. We would like to thank Leeds Inspired, the Walter Swan Trust, and Arts@Leeds for supporting earlier iterations of the Northern Short Story Festival Academy Project.

Thank you to Anna Chilvers for mentoring the writers, SJ Bradley for instigating and starting the project, and to Niccola Swan and Fiona Gell for all of their support.

'Beanz N Eggs' by Glenis Burgess was previously published in *The Colours of Life* anthology from Spilt Ink in 2022.

'Meeting Others Safely Outdoors' by Monica Dickson was previously published in *Funny Pearls*, an online journal dedicated to showcasing humour by women.

An earlier version of 'Woven Together in the Depths of the Earth' was highly commended in the Sean O'Faolain Short Story Prize 2019.

Child of Thought

Walter Swan

Transient I am, sliding.
Without strength. Gliding.
Mutable and changing.
Attempting, arranging
New faces, expressions.
Distracting digressions.
Escaping depressions.
Days pass as the bare recollections of bare thought,
Bloodless battles left unrecorded and fought
Between victors and vanquished anonymous.
All thoughts an amalgam, unseen, ambiguous,
Diverging, converging, together, apart.
One mind in one body with only one heart,
Yet thinking, resolving, convictions for my health,
Later ignored by a different myself
Who is yet the same who had forgotten it –
Abandoned child of he who had begotten it.
A child born from the body,
Not from the brain, gives hope to me.
One who will remember, holding hands,
Through into posterity. Thus stands,
Forever, love of generation, fixed in life,
Enshrined in love of woman, lover, wife.
Child, you are my permanent emotion
Among sliding thoughts and motion.

Foreword

Niccola Swan

In 2014 the Walter Swan Trust was established to celebrate the memory of Walter Swan (1954–2014) and to encourage new creative writing. The Trust is delighted to be supporting the publication of this second exciting anthology, in partnership with the Northern Short Story Festival and the Leeds Big Bookend Festival, SJ Bradley and Fiona Gell, with workshop leader, Anna Chilvers, and with Valley Press.

Walter was passionate about writing and encouraging others to be creative, which he did throughout his life and particularly through his teaching and theatre directing. He wrote short stories, poetry, plays, screenplays, and also published regular articles as a freelance journalist. He began work on two novels and has three published non-fiction books. He was naturally very collaborative and often wrote with others; his recent writing partner was Yvette Huddleston, with whom Walter worked for a number of years.

The common themes throughout Walt's life were kindness, warmth and humour. He was always sociable and had a great talent for friendship. Much of his time was dedicated to others as a family member, friend, teacher and director, and he provided support, encouragement and inspiration in each of these roles. Many people remember fondly his enthusiastic encouragement and support, whether with their own original writing or with their acting.

Walt was passionate about creative writing of all genres and, although he was very talented in his own right, it is his enthusiasm for the work of others which is the legacy that the Walter Swan Trust now aims to continue. He would have been delighted to be associated with this special book.

Foreword

SJ Bradley

In 2017, thanks to funding from the Arts@Leeds scheme and with support from the Walter Swan Trust, I helped run the first ever intake of the Northern Short Story Festival Academy scheme. Twelve new short story writers were selected to work together in groups of six, for a period of mentoring with Anna Chilvers, who has been involved with the scheme ever since.

Since that first intake, thirty writers have now gone through the programme.

The Northern Short Story Festival Academy scheme started as a product of frustration. I knew there were some incredibly talented writers in the region, but that there were few or no development opportunities to support them, and so I suggested to Fiona Gell of Leeds Lit Fest that we start and run our own development programme. Writers would submit to a simple application process, and those who were selected would go through a period of professional and craft development, supported by Anna Chilvers, with Fiona and I giving additional help when needed.

Writers have spoken warmly about their involvement in the scheme, with many of the participants from early intakes going on to sign book deals, have work commissioned for the BBC, or be included in Bloomsbury's *Test Signal* anthology. These success stories speak to how the programme is able to recognise and incubate new writing talent, without the barriers to entry that exist for other writing programmes. It is testament to all that, and to the dedication of Fiona Gell and Anna Chilvers, and to the strength of talent in the North, that you're holding this book in your hands now. I must say thank you to both, and to Niccola from the Walter Swan Trust, for their support in developing these new writers.

Eighteen brilliant writers have contributed short stories to this book, and no two are the same. The stories range from playful and experimental to folk horror to fantasy and remixed fairy tales. One of the groups underwent their mentoring over Zoom during the pandemic, and a couple of the stories speak directly to the strangeness of living through such seismic and life-altering times. Others speak of the body-altering horror of motherhood, or yearn for the freedom and wildness of the Scottish highlands.

It's been a joy to work on this book, and to find out that there is apparently no exhausting the well of talent in the North. I hope you enjoy it too.

Ototicular Dust

LMA Bauman-Milner

O-to-ti-cu-lar dust: (n., orig. unknown) mythical poison. Application methods: topical, inhalant, ingest, inject into flesh, eyes or ears. Full dosage is fatal, though what constitutes 'full dosage' is unknown. The effects may vary. Exposure can result in – and is not limited to – blindness due to eyes exploding, baldness, sudden flaying of skin from flesh, melting skeletal structure, liquefaction of select organs. Prior to death, victims emit a prolonged ululation. There only certainty is that it will cause pain: excruciating, eye-melting, soul-bombing pain.

They call me Biscuit, which suits me fine; makes me seem harmless and cuddly, like a gran who bakes for you and pinches your cheeks. This was always a good way to inspire trust, because I reminded them of their gran. I loved to bake, but I've stopped pinching cheeks. Too many memories; I have to be careful of the triggers. Cheeks never were a good way to estimate weight for roasting; invariably the meat would be overdone, rendered inedible. Leaning in close to pinch gave the chance to smell and be smelled; lavender and cookies were the best lure for unsuspecting children, and I could tell if they were at their best roasting age even with one whiff.

What can I say? It's a gift.

Now the story of how Roscoe and I ended up in a penthouse condo in the posh end of Waterloo, Ontario is probably less interesting than how Roscoe and I met in the first place. I had dragged my charred body from the wood-burning oven, and was resting on my back in a clearing out of sight of my cottage, groaning. That little bitch took me by surprise, and I was plotting a personalised vengeance for her. I had sloughed the worst of the charred skin, watched it drift on the breeze. But groaning and plotting were my priority.

I didn't notice the scent of blood at first. It was the sudden grip of claws around my leg that shocked me out of my torpor.

Still sluggish, I crawled around the clearing trying to shake off the claws. It took a few moments to sink in that the clawed forearm wasn't attached to anything except my leg. Woozy, I stood and turned to survey the rest of the clearing, until I spotted a heap of carnage at the far edge, near the tree-line. As I approached, I saw the wolf's head was still attached to a cross-section of torso, but its eyes rolled madly and its tongue trailed in the grass. Crouching next to it, I examined the wound that had severed its body. It was a mostly-clean cut, not too many ragged bits. I whistled through the gap in my own teeth, long and low, as I considered whether or not to help.

I reached down and yanked the paw from my leg, held it out like a peace offering. 'Here. I think this is yours.'

The wolf turned towards me, and I could see the effort it cost him not to succumb to the hideous pain. I watched as his eyes crossed a little to focus on the proffered limb. He looked back at me and his panting changed in timbre and tone, gathered together with huge gaps of rhythmic sound as he sucked air down into his almost-ruined lungs.

He was laughing.

It took most of the afternoon to collect the errant bits of the wolf. That Woodsman was getting more vicious with every telling. Before, he used to just eviscerate the wolf to free the women; this vivisection was pure rage and an act more evil than even the worst of us could devise.

Because of our histories, Roscoe and I had a particular fascination with children; we couldn't resist toying with them before destroying them. Took us years to unlearn that downfall. We were both fighting the triggers. How could we predict the condo complex would regrade from 'active retirement community' to 'family-friendly luxury living'? I guess the older neighbours were dying off.

Nothing to do with us, let me be clear on that. We had learned to let well enough alone and just live. When I took Roscoe out for walkies, we stayed away from playgrounds. During the summer, we went out late at night, avoiding the known hook-up spots. As the years passed, I couldn't muster the strength to hold Roscoe back, especially on full moon nights; my hips would grind and I'd be in agony for days. We conceded defeat by our third century together, and we stayed in on full moon nights.

Hallowe'en was our favourite holiday. Though the neighbours' kids gave us a wide berth for the rest of the year, they couldn't wait to be terrified by our hallway. We always won for best decorations in the building, but after the tenth year, we deferred the prize to whomever came second. The superintendent chose to act as bouncer for our floor, counting children off and on the lift. I suspected there was a taint of Woodsman in his blood, but apart from that level black gaze, I couldn't be certain. Roscoe avoided him entirely – didn't like the way the hair on the back of his neck twitched whenever the super came near.

I knew something was wrong. A low moan registered on the cusp of hearing and I thought it was the wind. Smiling and handing out candied apple treats to the bravest witches and demons, I was distracted and dismissed it. I wasn't sure I had heard it through the shouts and giggles of hyper-stimulated relief of teens and tweenies. When the last wave of children ebbed back toward the elevator, I rolled up from my evil witch hunch, holding the empty tray, dotted with oozing circles of caramel. I touched a finger to the sweet stickiness and brought it to my mouth – even after all these years, I still have a sweet tooth.

Roscoe's furred hand captured mine before the caramel touched my lips. I hadn't heard him come up behind me. He joined me in the doorway, still holding my hand. Grinning, his teeth stretched out as his mask slipped, almost revealing his muzzle. He reached up with his free hand and smoothed his features into blank humanness. Roscoe stared down the hallway, towards the elevator and the superintendent standing guard. That vengeful smile crept onto his face.

'You didn't.'

'Shhh.'

'Tell me you didn't.'

'Just a little. A pinch, and nothing more.'

'You pillock.'

Roscoe snorted, tongue lolling. 'I wanted to test it.'

'You had to test it on all of the neighbours' kids? You've quite possibly destroyed everything we've worked for.'

That low moan swelled as more children slumped over in the hallway, and one or two were sick. The super moved from child to child, sitting them upright against the walls and wiping chins as needed. He glared at us every time he moved.

'I said it was only a pinch. And boiling it in the sugar probably reduced its efficacy.'

'Probably?' I couldn't keep the fear from raising my voice. 'Stupid mutt, you haven't a clue what to do in the kitchen.'

Roscoe gazed at me, searching my face. His nose twitched. 'Stupid witch, you're more miffed that I fucked around with your recipe than you are about the kids.'

'There's no need to be vulgar about it,' I sniffed. 'I hope you've got the antidote ready.'

Roscoe moved back into the condo. 'Super's on his way. You take care of it. Spin it as tummy aches all round, and there's at least one slightly wormy apple in the bunch for authenticity.' He took the tray from me. 'I'll go wash the rest of the evidence away.'

I pulled the fake warty nose down, let it dangle from its elastic. It bobbed like a bizarre goitre in front of my throat. I swallowed compulsively, tasting the children's fear and vomit in the air. The super marched towards me, the oblong light from the elevator bordering his silhouette.

His eyes flared red as he drew closer; it must be the flashing lights strung along the walls. The lights between us flared to blinding brightness, then popped into oblivion. I blinked the afterimages away, straining to focus on the backlit figure as he closed in.

He is the Woodsman. Shit.

I stepped back in shock, forgetting for a moment who I am and that *he* is not my villain.

The first of the ululating cries – weak, thready, filled with pain – burbled from the farthest end of the hallway, dragged from the throat of a child, shredding vocal cords. The scent of fear in the hallway shifted as the children edged to their ototicular ends. Every death has its own smell: musty flowers for consumption, fresh cut hay for broken bones, cinnamon rolls for being burned alive. I hadn't smelt this death before; it was rich and mellow, full of sugar and grace, pierced with a fruity tang.

I couldn't help myself, even when the Woodsman stopped in front of me. I breathed deep, and my smile slid in the streams of saliva drooling from the corners of my mouth, dripping from the crooked false nose beneath. I smiled at the Woodsman, ready to savour the scent of his death.

He stepped back and I grinned wider as he glanced over his shoulder. I could see that he was faltering, uncertain whether to confront me or comfort the children. That smell, now laced with vanilla, grew stronger, and I stepped forward as I inhaled the heavenly scent.

The Woodsman stepped back again, unnerved by my audacity. His eyes flared red again, but I did not care. 'Not my villain,' I hissed, moving away from the safety of the doorway. He looked left and right as he moved back towards the elevator, deciding which children to save, which were too far gone. He ducked and darted to his right, reaching out to grab a fairy princess slumped against the wall, her dress stained with grey vomit. I hissed and lunged at him, and he staggered back, abandoning the girl. I matched him, herding him back, feinting at him every time he tried to be the hero.

'Not my villain.'

Every time I said this, he seemed smaller. The scent of that ototicular death increased as the children drifted closer to the border; I felt light-headed, drunk, and oh-so-ready for a feast. I couldn't wait any longer.

With the Woodsman reduced to a mere superintendent again, I hunkered down next to a Mighty Ninja Power Mutant, my body shifting into its natural shape of humps and crooks. I inhaled, through the fake nose too, sucked the smells deep into my lungs, and my saliva ran red in anticipation of gorging.

I sneezed.

Lemongrass and pepper cut sharp through the air, an arrow through the heart of the impending deaths.

I growled and turned back towards my door. *Who dares?*

Roscoe advanced, pausing at each child to trickle a stream of sparkling powder into its ear. He glanced at me and shook his head, tutting at the sight. 'Look at yourself, Biscuit. Who's bolloxing our hard work now?' With every dose, sharp citrus and black pepper cut through my nostrils, and my eyes streamed. That delicious death faded as the children revived, coughing and spitting out gobs of golden mucus, threaded with black.

I pinched my nose shut, tore the fake one from my neck and threw it away. It bounced and rolled, coming to a jerky rest at the edge of the elevator. The super sat in a corner, knees curled up to his chest. He stared wide-eyed as the rubber nose twitched, sneezed, and was still. The super looked up, his eyes fixed on nothing. His gibbering laugh heralded his mind's permanent holiday.

Roscoe blew the last of the antidote into the last child's ear, and dusted his hands clean. He peered into the elevator, still wary of his ancient villain. I resumed my disguise of matronly granny. Roscoe grinned at me, leaned in and turned the panel key back to auto, pressed 'G' and stepped back as the doors closed. 'We don't want the kids to go back to Mommy and Daddy with that hot mess of weirdness, do we?' He jangled the super's keys from one finger. 'We'll just open the stairs and make sure they all get home safe, eh?'

The children behind us staggered to their feet, asking groggy questions. The littler ones wailed and clung to the nearest teens, keeping as far from us as possible. With assurances from Roscoe that it must have been a bad batch of apples, the kids shuffled through the stairwell door.

For the rest of the night, Roscoe and I cleared up the mess and smell of death in the hallway, scrubbing until no trace of what occurred remained.

I don't open the door on Hallowe'en anymore. I honestly don't know what Roscoe was thinking, doing that to the neighbours' kids. We were thinly thanked for administering ipecac to all the affected children, but the condo's board insisted that we never participated in the building's Hallowe'en festivities again. A slap on the wrist for the use of ototicular dust, and we were happy to accept that. If they did know, we'd have been lucky to escape with our heads attached to our necks, and our bowels in the correct place.

We've waited for more than half a century now, and we're certain the original neighbours' kids have moved on. No Hallowe'en for us ever again. But that's okay.

This year, we're introducing *Krampusnacht*.

Duckie

John Biglands

Duckie stands in the corner of the office, watching me as always. At least, I think he's watching me. I don't like to think about what kind of face lies hidden under that black hood, what kind of eyes watch me from its shadow. I've never seen them, or any other part of Duckie for that matter. I presume he has arms and legs, hands and feet, but they don't see the light of day. To me, Duckie is just a big, black cloak hanging over some unknown body. A dark, hooded angel watching me, making sure I never forget.

Why's he called Duckie? Well, I call him that because the bus driver did. It was the first day I went back to work after Suzie died. Duckie stood in line behind me in the bus queue, creating a gap between me and the woman standing beside me with her eyes glued to her phone. The bus pulled up and the doors opened. I knew the bus driver, or at least I recognised him. I'd seen him every working day for the last ten years, but I'd never said more to him than "Return to Hanley, please" and "Cheers mate."

Anyway, that driver knew me. At least well enough to know there was something different. Perhaps he'd heard about Suzie, or perhaps he just saw it in my face. I don't know.

"You alright, Duckie?" he said.

I wasn't alright. I was empty and sad and tired of being alive, but I wasn't going to tell him that. I looked up to say, "fine thanks," but he wasn't looking at me. I turned, and there behind me was Duckie, silent and ominous as always. I don't know if the bus driver actually saw him that day, but it was the first time it felt like someone else recognised this thing I take with me everywhere. I've called him Duckie ever since.

I've grown used to having Duckie around. Sometimes,

I almost forget he's there. At work, engrossed in some spreadsheet or email exchange, I'll look up and realise for a short, heart-skipping moment that I don't know where he is. But then I spot him, standing by the water cooler or the lift doors. I don't think anyone else sees him. No one ever mentions him. But I've seen people take side steps to avoid walking into him when he was standing between the cubicles. And the other day I saw Tom from Media, cup in hand and halfway to the coffee machine, make a U-turn because Duckie was standing in front of it.

It's the work's Christmas do tonight and Duckie stays very close. I'm standing at the bar in a crowded nightclub holding a coke. I already had a glass of wine at the meal and Suzie never liked me to drink too much. I lean against the bar and watch the mush of people gyrating on the dance floor. I'll show due diligence. Two drinks should do it. Then I'll leave. Should be home by eleven.

Some of our lot are already half-cut. Bob from Finance is headbanging to 'Christmas Time' by The Darkness. The girls from his department are laughing as he flails his limbs around with all the grace and coordination of a newborn elephant... It makes me smile. I like Bob. We used to go for a drink after work sometimes, but I don't really speak to him these days.

Ali from HR is trying to make her way across the dance-floor. I watch her progress as she sidesteps swivelling hips and flailing elbows. She arrives safely at a space at the bar just next to me, red-faced and sweating. I don't fancy her chances of making it back to her table with an armful of drinks. She smiles at me and I smile back. Ali sent me a card when Suzie died asking if I wanted to talk. I never replied, but it was kind of her all the same.

"Hey, Ed," she says.

"Hey."

"It's nice to see you out."

I nod. I was never a great talker, even when I had Suzie. The barman walks to our end of the bar and Ali waves.

She leans so far forward that her feet leave the ground as she tries to attract his attention. "Three pints of Guinness and a G and T, love," she yells.

I look back across the dance floor. Duckie's there. The only stationary body in the melée surrounding him. They're playing Ibiza tunes now and the strobes are on. The movement of the dancers becomes jerky as the lights flash so that they look like stick men in a child's flick-book. In the split second blinks of darkness between the flashes, Duckie disappears. I like that. I like the thought that Duckie could disappear. I feel a hand on my arm. Ali's talking to me.

"How are you bearing up?"

I feel a panic rise inside me. I look at her blankly.

"Since Suzie I mean."

The mention of Suzie's name still jolts me. I almost snatch my arm away.

"Let us know if you ever need to talk," she says.

I look down at the small hand on my sleeve. Maybe it's because Ali's so small, or because of the way she's looking at me, but I'm not angry at her. I resist the urge to walk away. She's trying to help.

"Thanks," I say, "but I don't think I can."

"That's alright love." She rubs my arm. "Well, you know where I am. Any time." She smiles and scoops up the four glasses from the bar in her tiny hands, pressing them against her ample chest ready for her journey back across the dancefloor. I still can't believe she'll make it through the morass of drunken dancers with her drinks intact.

I look out across the dancefloor, reeling a little from the emotional livewire that Ali's just touched inside me. I spot Duckie, motionless and silent, standing next to Julie and Dave from IT who are throwing shapes at each other in increasingly suggestive ways. They seem unaware of his presence, but they never venture too close to him. It's as though he's surrounded by an invisible force-field that they cannot cross. I spot Ali again, shimmying and twisting her way through the crowd, still protectively clutching her brood of drinks against her chest. She sees the little island of space around Duckie, and moves towards it. I watch, intrigued. When will she change course? When will that part of Duckie that repels people kick in and divert her? He stands still. She reaches the edge of his island of space. I can't tell if he's looking at her or not. A dancer nudges Ali and she takes a sudden step towards Duckie, shifting her weight expertly to stop the drinks from spilling.

And then it happens.

Duckie moves. He just slides sideways like a mannequin on a conveyor belt. I jump up from my barstool. There are no signs of limbs moving under Duckie's cloak. His whole body just drifts across the dancefloor. He moves towards Julie and Dave who both step away. Dave accidentally elbows the new lad from Accounting in the ribs, who turns around to glare at him. Dave waves both hands in apology. Ali continues across the dance floor, oblivious to the monumental feat she's achieved. How did she do that?

*

I find Ali's house easily enough. It's an ordinary mid-terrace with an extraordinarily bright yellow door and multi-coloured stained glass in the bay window. I check the number painted on the stone wall fronting her house, but I already know it's Ali's place. I saw Duckie standing in the small front garden as soon as I turned into the street. I don't know if he approves of what I'm doing or not, but he seems to know where I'm going.

I, on the other hand, am absolutely sure that this is a huge mistake. Whatever impulse possessed me to find Ali at the end of the Christmas party and agree to talk to her has long left me behind. Why did I do it? Because she made Duckie move? So what? What am I going to say to her? I'm not ready to talk about Suzie. I don't know how.

As soon as I knock, a dog starts to bark. The door opens and a hunched over Ali beckons me in, one hand on the door handle the other gripping the collar of a young labrador whose claws scrabble against the wooden floors as he tries to get to me. I can't tell if his intentions are friendly or not.

"Come in, come in!" shouts Ali above the dog's barking. "S'alright, he's friendly. Just a bit over-enthusiastic. Calm down Hector, ya big idiot!!"

"Er, ok," I say, sidling past the dog.

She closes the door and lets go of the animal, who immediately gallops up to me, takes a couple of sniffs at my groin and then trots back to Ali.

"Maniac," she says as she rubs his head. "Fancy a cuppa, Ed?"

"Er, yeah ok. Do you have coffee?"

"Sure. Go through to the front room, I'll bring 'em in."

By the time she brings in the drinks I'm sitting on one of Ali's large couches. She sits down across from me, folds her legs underneath her, and blows steam from a gargantuan mug of tea. Duckie's sitting next to her, the darkness of his cloak almost comical against the yellow sofa. Hector trots into the room, his muscular tail thumping the wooden door as he passes. He takes one look at Duckie, gives a quiet whine and walks out again.

"Mad dog," says Ali, shaking her head. "Enjoy the party, Ed?"

"Er yeah, I suppose." I shuffle on the couch. "Well not really, no. I'm not very good at that sort of thing."

She smiles. "Yeah."

I'm starting to feel hot. I wish I hadn't come.

She takes a sip of her tea. "So you wanted to talk about your Suzie?"

It feels too quick, too blunt. I hear myself sucking breath between my teeth. "I'm sorry, Ali I shouldn't have... I'm not sure..." I look into my coffee mug and try to steady my breathing. "I'm really sorry, but I don't know if I can do this. I think maybe it's too soon for me."

Ali rubs the side of her mug with her hand and shakes her

head. "Don't worry, love," she says, "don't you worry."

Duckie has moved closer to her and he seems to have grown. Her head doesn't even reach his shoulder now. I wonder how she can look so comfortable with him looming over her like that. She seems oblivious. She takes a sip of her tea. "Did you know that I lost someone too?"

I shake my head. "I'm sorry."

One rainbow socked foot disappears under Ali's thigh. "Yeah. My partner, Iain. Cancer. Three years now."

"I'm so sorry."

She pushes both palms into her face and wipes them sideways. Her breath shudders a little as she takes it in. She doesn't apologise. "S'a bitch init?" she says.

I envy her, her tears. It seems strange to me that she can cry so easily. Duckie stares at me. I wonder again what kind of face is hidden beneath his hood. If I pulled it back, what colour eyes would I find staring at me. Suddenly, I want to tell Ali about him. I have a yearning to tell her about this darkness that follows me so relentlessly.

"There's this thing." I begin.

Ali sniffs and wipes her eyes again. She gives me a smile and nods.

"It's like this big, dark creature." I glance at Duckie. He doesn't move. "It's always there, this thing. It follows me around. It's not like it scares me. Not exactly. Sometimes it almost feels like a friend. But, because it's always there, I feel like I can't really live very well. It's as though everything has been painted grey. Everything is lifeless. And I'm left just going through the motions. I can get up, I can go to work, I can cook meals. I can even go to Christmas parties. But it's like, when he's there, someone has put a muffler on life, and I can't really feel anything."

I don't know what I expect Ali to do. Will she realise that I'm going mad? Will she be scared of me? Will she ask me to leave? But she doesn't do any of those things.

"Yes, it is like that," she says, nodding. "It's just like that."

Of all the things she could have said, nothing could be more perfect. I release a long sigh. I hadn't realised I was holding my breath. "You felt like that too?"

"I used to feel like there was this big, black dog that followed me around. It felt as though, if there was anything good, anything fun in the world, then that dog would just growl and scare it away."

I stare at Duckie. He's standing further away now, by the bookcase. I didn't see him move. I wrap my hands around my coffee cup. I want to ask Ali if she ever actually saw the dog. How real was it? But I can't. I'm too scared.

"How did you get rid of it, your dog?" I ask.

She shakes her head. "I don't think you can get rid of it."

"But you seem so... I dunno, sorted. Normal."

"Normal?" Ali laughs. "You don't know me very well, do you?" She uncrosses one leg and massages her toes. "I'm not normal. I don't think I really want to be."

"But you seem happy. Or at least ok?"

"I'm doing ok. I have my down days, but on the whole, yeah. I'm living again."

"How did you...?" I realise I'm about to ask her the same question. I pause, searching for words. "What I mean is, how did you learn to live with it, your dog thing?"

Ali looks past me, at the wall behind the couch. "I accepted him," she says. "Grief, anger, all that stuff. You can't get rid of it. It's a part of me now, always will be. So, I started to try to work out how to be with him, instead of being scared. I bought Hector. My friends thought I was crazy, but I knew that if I had a tangible thing like a puppy to look after that I'd have to engage. I needed something that I'd have to love and train." She laughs. "Well, sort of train. I dunno. Somehow it helped. It wasn't until after I'd had him a few weeks that I realised that Hector was also a big, black dog. He wasn't so big those days, mind."

"And did it?"

"Sorry?"

"Did it help?"

She nods. "Yeah, it helped. Hector's a gigantic pain in the arse sometimes, but he's lovely. I haven't actually seen my other dog for a while now."

"You saw it then? You actually saw this dog? It was real to you?"

I recognise the expression on her face so well. The fear of what I might think if I see the craziness inside her. I feel ashamed of my question, but I really need to know the answer. She takes in a big breath and then nods her head. Tiny, quick movements, more resolve than answer.

"Yes," she says, "I used to see him. Still do on bad days." Her eyes look wet again. "Still think I'm normal?"

At first, my tears are all about Ali. I see this tiny, brave woman trying to cope alone with her grief and loss and it breaks me. It feels as though the faceless cruelty of the world will push every last gasp of air from my lungs. And then, of course, it's not about Ali anymore. It's about Suzie, and it's about me. All that I lost, and all the things we never did together, and never will. The pain, the guilt, the anger. It all comes rushing out in a hot, noisy mess. Involuntary and resisted, the sobs come in great, ugly spasms, constricting my throat and bursting out of me like exorcised demons.

Ali's beside me, her hand on my back now, warm between my shoulder blades. She's saying things but I don't hear her words. All I can say is, "I'm sorry." I say it over and over again and each time it means a different thing. I'm sorry for crying on her couch. I'm sorry for all that the world has wrung from this kind, brave little woman. And I'm sorry for my own pain. How I wish it had never been, and how I wish it had not turned me into such a cold, useless hermit.

I feel her arm around my shoulders. I hear the soft thump of Hector's head pushing open the lounge door, and the click of his claws as he walks across the wooden floor. He lies down by my feet. I can't see Duckie. I don't look for him.

Ali drives me out to the Peak District after work. Her ancient yellow Citroen 2cv struggles up the steep hills, threatening to overheat. Hector lies on the back seat, his head on his paws, looking dolefully up at me whenever I turn round. He hates the car, the engine's too loud. I watch the scenery pass by in silence. It's spring and the land is purple with heather.

We park up and walk across the moors. Ali tells me about her day. How she's behind on her reports and how she got told off for being too informal in a meeting with the directors. I begin to feel indignant for her, but there's no point. She doesn't care. She's already laughing about it. The bracken is high and Hector bounds through it. I catch momentary glimpses of his head above the foliage. He looks like some strange, black dolphin breaching a green sea.

We have our picnic at the top of a hill. I pull Ali's tartan blanket from my rucksack. She takes out a flask of hot water and starts making tea in a pair of rainbow striped mugs. I show her some pencil drawings I've done of Duckie. I haven't drawn since my school days, and the perspective's not quite right. His head's too big. But it felt good to do them.

"They're really good," says Ali, tilting her head as looks at them. She mashes a teabag against the side of the mug and hands it to me. "He's kind of cute."

"Cute?"

"Well, you know. Maybe not cute, but he looks a bit sad, bless him. Like he needs a love."

I shake my head. "You're bonkers."

"Yep," she says, balancing her mug on her knees, "stark raving. Shame I'm not as well-balanced and rational as you."

It feels good to laugh. I look down the hill to the line of trees that mark the edge of the woods. Duckie's standing next to the stile that we'll climb over when we head back. He's quite far away but it's definitely him. That's ok. I'm used to him now. He doesn't ruin things.

I'm trying to think of something to say to Ali. Something that will make her laugh again. I see Duckie move. At least he seems to move. It's hard to tell. There's a lopsidedness to his cloak as though he's put his hand on something. I lean forward and squint my eyes. There's some shorter, dark thing beside him. I stand up so I can see better. It's a dog. I can't tell what breed but it's huge. Perhaps an Irish wolfhound, but bigger and jet-black. I can't make out its eyes through the shaggy mane. Duckie's arm is outstretched, his hand invisible, buried in the thick hair of the beast, and they stand there together, watching us.

The Death of the Author

Lucy Brighton

You sit down to write. You are in your writing shed surrounded by your favourite things. You open a word document. You minimise ChatGPT with its enticing "send a message…"
You begin to write.

I'm back, back where it all started. Other than a layer of dust, the house hasn't changed in the past five years. The smell of cigarettes still hangs in the air. I take the stairs two at a time, telling myself it can't be – I can't be here. The house was sold years ago. But I'm here. I'm touching the banister and feeling the worn thread of the carpet beneath my feet.

I near the bottom of the stairs and strain to hear. She can't be there. She's dead, I know it in my mind, but a lingering swell of hope pushes me around the corner and into the living room. I'm half expecting my mother to be sitting in the corner, one leg tucked under her, smoking a cig, and complaining we don't visit enough.

Instead, her absence fills the room.

You stop. You have written yourself into a corner. Where is this going? You drown under the unyielding fear of failure. You remember the invitation. Send a message…

WHAT HAPPENS NEXT?

I stand there, in the middle of the empty living room, feeling a sense of disorientation wash over me. How did I get here? Why did I come back to this house, this place that holds so many painful memories?

I take a deep breath, trying to push away the thoughts and emotions that threaten to overwhelm me. I need to focus on the present, on what's in front of me.

You thank the AI overlord. Of course, it all makes sense now. You think about the room. You need to consider what is out of place. You admonish yourself for giving in to the twinkling dots promising that sweet elixir. Why worry, it asks you, why tie yourself up in knots?

Her black cup filled with tea and a tot of whisky sits beside the sofa. I touch it: cold. Of course it is. I take a deep breath and ask myself if there is any possibility this is real. I look at my hand where a wedding ring has been for the past two years. My finger is naked.

The sound of Rod Stewart drifts into the room. I follow the music and find her varnished wooden rocking chair groaning along to the music from the record player. I move slowly to the sound system, wondering why my senses insist on deceiving me. The plastic is spinning too slowly, the needle jumping back, playing the same circle over and over.

You can almost hear it calling you. "I can finish that for you." You refuse to listen. You are quite capable of writing this story yourself. You managed it before this infernal AI made everything so easy.

You wait, proud of your resolve. You wait longer. Maybe a couple of lines you think, definitely no more than that.

WHAT HAPPENS NEXT?

I frown at the record player, feeling a wave of confusion wash over me. This is impossible. My mother passed away five years ago. I saw her take her last breath, held her hand until it went cold. I know she's not here. And yet, everything in this room tells me otherwise.

I take a step back, trying to make sense of it all. That's when I notice something odd about the photograph on the wall. It's a picture of my mother, my father, and me, taken when I was a child. But there's someone else in the picture now, someone who wasn't there before. A young woman, with long brown hair and a bright smile. I don't recognize her.

"Yes, I see," you declare and start tapping the keys again.

I pinch myself, like they do in all good scary stories. I watch my skin whiten and then flush pink. I sit in the chair and the house sighs with relief. It hugs me and soaks me back into its bricks.

The music jumps and then stops but I think I can hear humming. The same tune, just out of earshot. I rock gently and close my eyes. Yes, humming low and melodic. Her favourite song. I whisper some of the words to the house and it warms and settles. Is she here? Did the house never let her go?

The sight of her pallid, lifeless face, mouth agape appears unbidden behind my eyelids. That was real, so this can't be. This house will be filled with the songs of a new family. I open my eyes expecting to see the bedroom I share with my husband. I expect to feel the calming warmth of his skin against mine. I expect to leave this place once and for all.

The humming gets louder, and I see her in the shadows cast by the breach of the morning light.

"Mum?"

She doesn't move.

I get up from the chair and move towards her.

"Mum, where have you been?"

She steps out into the light, her face still twisted in the throes of dying.

"Here," she says, "waiting for you to visit."

We can't have the same corpse twice

Kate Burke

I was still alive when the phone rang. Dry spit clogged the corners of my mouth and made my voice thick. It was half past five in the morning.

What?

"Do you want to earn one hundred and forty six pounds forty five today?"

Yeah? Why are you crying?

I staggered to the bus stop, bag bashing into my knee. I lurched into a free seat and eventually caught my breath. A crumbly man beside me shuffled towards the window. I tried to calm pink cheeks with the back of my hand. I licked the salt from my top lip.

As soon as I arrived at the studio, Maisie bundled me through the corridor and into a fluorescently lit, mirrored room with no windows. An earpiece perched precariously between her temple and helix. Teetering. She was definitely going to cry again soon.

"Thanks so much, Morgan. Lifesaver, honestly."

Not much I won't do for one hundred and forty six pounds forty five.

Three people were responsible for making me look dead. I said that was overkill, and they didn't laugh. They slicked my hair away from my head and applied a grey paste to my brow. My skin was cold from the paint, but for flutters of warm breath as their dabbing and blending became more precise. Maisie burst in.

"Is she ready? Oliver wants her in five..." A little gasp.

I understood the gasp when I saw a reflection of the dead girl. Her black eyes were shrunken behind jagged cheekbones; sallow skin barely tissued over soon-to-be-rotten flesh. Unearthly green seeped into the pallor of her neck, her hair was soggy and smeared with mud and leaves. She smelt of cold moss and clods of wet earth. Cracked, grimy fingers raised to touch her beatless heart, but they were smacked away by her creator.

I floated behind Maisie into a dark room with a blindingly bright centre. Figures lurked in shadows, sleek machines scattered around the central focus: a shining, stainless steel table and a white bloke in a white coat. Maisie halted and stood desperately behind a man in baggy jeans and a striped t-shirt.

"Oh, she's good, where did we find her?"

"She lives in my spare room."

Busy heads turned, but I didn't care because I was dead.

I lay motionless on the slab. The lights, blaring at the corpse from the rig above, should have felt hot but they didn't. I basked in my death, as the detective consulted with the pathologist about the cause of my demise, options for which there were many. In between takes, I remained. There were three scenes with the dead girl, and a tight schedule, so it was favourable to just stay put. I was the best stiff the gaffer had ever seen.

"Wrap on scene five!"

"Thanks, Morgan."

I was peeled from the table and wrapped in a gown, the bristles sharp against my slimy skin. I trailed after Maisie, back to the dressing room with no windows. The shower was running.

Washing away the surface of my death was strange. Though the paint was gone, grey remained. My feet were numb against the ground and everything felt far away. It was completely obvious to me I was still dead. Silence dwelled in my cadaver. The warmth of my blood was gone. Maisie carted me out of the studio, and I waited quietly for the bus. I sat alone and drifted back to Maisie's spare room.

Fuck, I'm dead.

Away from the morgue, I felt nothing. I stood against the open freezer for a while. Maisie arrived and wondered if we had any ice for her gin.

When the show aired, we were slumped on the sofa amongst an array of organised fun and our friends. Some of them had turned up dressed like corpses. They were clearly still alive.

"The gaffer said she's the best stiff he'd ever seen."

"High praise, Morgan. Can't wait to see your debut."

And there it was. My dead body. I poured over my cold lips, lifeless shoulders, hollow face. I looked radiant and I felt perfect. Departing friends told me my performance was outstanding, they were moved to tears, and they would like a mention in the acceptance speech when I inevitably received an Oscar. I laughed politely and waited for them to go away. Maisie sighed once they did.

"You need to submit your invoice, Morgan."

Breakfast seemed completely pointless. So did all the other meals. If Maisie was around I'd join in because it was probably hard enough living with a corpse without them staring at you as you ate. There was a pretence I had with Maisie where I had to behave like I wasn't dead. I thought she'd feel responsible if she found out, and her life was emotional enough without such a burden. She had an allotted time for crying, which was usually between nine and twenty-past, upon her return home from work. Once that was over, she would have a shower, come back in, make a double gin and tonic and say, "fucking Oliver". Spending time with Maisie always felt like she was lamenting at my grave, which now, of course, she was.

I asked Maisie if Oliver might need me to come and be a corpse again.

"We only needed you because the agency let us down. Besides, we can't have the same corpse twice."

I didn't know there was an agency for corpses. I stole her laptop when she was at work and went back to my tomb. The next day, Sharon (from the agency) called me. She thought it might be an issue that I didn't have access to a car, but she'd like to put me on her books since I already had a professional credit. I said I'd only do work where they needed a stiff, which Sharon found strange.

In four months, I'd been dead three times and turned down a walk on part in Hollyoaks twice. Sharon barked that most young women would jump at the chance for Hollyoaks, and it's *not the done thing* for background artists to turn down work. I said I wasn't a background artist, I was a dead woman trying to pay her rent.

Each time I opened my eyes and saw my ashen skin and bloodless body, I felt as I was meant to. I would stagger to the field in which I perished, or slab to be examined, or bathroom where I'd overdosed, and savour my deceased truth until we wrapped. Nobody else ever looked as dead as me. I was euphoric in my extinction.

At the pub, our friends would be desperate to find out where I'd been dead. Maisie would look off to the side with a little pout until someone asked how her show was going.

"It is going amazingly well, thank you."

I'd watch everyone, warm blooded and flowing with wine, slinking between each other, sweat and breath mixing in the air. Nobody ever seemed to notice the stench emitting from my rotting lungs. Some boys seemed to like it. I took one home and asked them how it felt to fuck a dead girl. He said, "so good".

A stressed woman, who worked for Oliver and with Maisie, called to ask if I'd come back for season three.

I thought you couldn't have the same corpse twice?

"Well, you wouldn't be a corpse, you'd be alive."

Alive?

"DI Harper is being tortured by the ghosts of his past and is meeting the victims he's let down previously in everyday situations because it turns out the person originally convicted for murdering you in season one was actually innocent and it was his partner all along, you see, don't tell anyone that please, so we're trying to get all the old stiffs back for those scenes, then Oliver wants to do cutaways to the original episodes, blah blah. A continuity nightmare to be honest. Are you still brunette?"

Yeah.

"Perfect."

It was not perfect. I wasn't an actor, and I knew I'd do a bad job of being alive. Maisie said if I didn't do it she'd kick me out. It was unlikely anyone else would accept a free-lance corpse as a housemate. I reluctantly accepted the role.

I never slept, so I was on time to set off with Maisie at the crack of dawn. She drove silently with pursed lips all the way to the studio. The living me was supposed to serve DI Harper a pint at the bar, and flash him a youthful, innocent (yet knowing) smile. I was concerned my black-ened teeth would negate the impression. I didn't mention it. They didn't notice the skin flaying from my arms as I clambered into a denim jacket. They said nothing of the bald patches on my skull when they gathered my hair into a high ponytail. The buzz of blowflies followed me onto the location – a working man's club around the corner. For the first take, they asked me to pour a pint in the background. My fingertips started to slip away as I pulled on the tap. Degloving. Rotten skin floated in the froth.

I passed the pint over to DI Harper. His wide eyes met my dead ones. His face drained of colour and his throat contracted. Sweat prickled his forehead and I knew his stomach churned. I smiled and my jaw unhinged. Maggots fell from where my decomposing tongue had been. A belch of vomit rose in his throat.

"Cut! Amazing, Howard, well done."

Howard sprinted from his barstool. They found him outside trembling into a cigarette.

I loved being dead. I pitied the living; they were silly and tightly wound. I spent most of October on a farm, running after children in a live action Halloween horror experience. I didn't relish the wails and cries, but it was a small price to pay for the cold clod of earth pressed into my cheeks. I'd come home, caked in grave, and wait for my forlorn housemate to emerge. Maisie was working on a different show, but sleeping with Oliver, so he still made her cry. Through her tears she would ask me how I did it, how I was always so calm.

I'm dead, Maisie, nothing matters, it's tremendous.

By then, some of my bones were exposed and I would caress them at night. I was conscious of my necrotic smell, so I mostly stayed in.

One evening, Maise screamed "get out you fucking prick" at Oliver five times. The doors slammed, and she sniffled on her own. I sat for a while, haunting her spare room as she sobbed. Eventually I clambered out, skeleton prodding through the soles of my feet. I left pools of decay on the carpet. She curled into me on the sofa.

"You stink."

I know. It's the flesh.

Reruns of our drama played on the television. We snuggled together in silence watching the day I died.

"You make for a lovely corpse, Morgan."

Haha.

"Sorry I've been such a bitch to you."

I didn't think you had.

"I've thought a lot of bad thoughts. I always wanted to be an actor and now here you are, getting loads of work."

You're a great assistant production manager.

"I hate it. It makes me cry and it wasn't my plan."

I'm not really acting, I'm just being myself.

"You're brilliant."

You could be too, Maisie.

I called Sharon and, within a day, Maisie was on the books. She had access to a car, after all. As luck would have it, there was a music video shoot coming up for a goth metal band, and they were going to need a lot of young, beautiful corpses.

Maisie's knuckles were shaking. I squeezed her hand and left a glistening stain across her wrist. I sank into the chair as we transformed. When I opened my eyes, two dead girls gazed back at me in wonder.

Beanz 'n Eggs

Glenis Burgess

PART ONE – JACK
(with, *in italics,* his Mam in his head)

Jeeps, I wish I'd listened to me Mam. I reeeeeeally wish I'd listened to her. If I had, chances are I wouldn't be here scared out of me wits.

Wits. (I can hear her saying it.) *You've not got what I'd call wits, my lad. Just like your father* (always dabs her eyes here) *God rest his soul, ne'er-do well that he was, but a PLANNING man. But you, our Jack, you've not got the wits to plan anything. Where are you going to end up in life if you never plan? You listen to that Zack more than you listen to me, your own mother. Not on drugs, are you? Because if you are ... ?*

Drugs? Fat chance. I do listen to Zack more than to her – and why not? All I get from, her is nag, nag, plan, plan, wits, wits, all the ... wittering time. Now, Zack, best mate for life. Zack n' Jack 4 ever. We're not ... I mean, we're not ... I mean, we're just good mates. Whatever! Anyway, if I had listened to her, I wouldn't be here with this goose under me arm and I'm sure those eggs it laid're pure gold. They're heavy enough in me pockets, anyway.

Gold eggs. Gold eggs. (Jeeps, her voice is so loud I thought she was here with me.) *Yer daft lad.*

> "Fe, fi, fo fum
> I smell the blood of an Englishman
> eeer. Dun't rhyme ... eeer ... fi, fi fo fan
> nah that dun't work
> MUM, that's it. Fe, fi fo fum
> I smell the blood of an Englishmum
> Yeah, that's it. Definitely."

Did that giant say blood? Blood! Bloody loud, if you ask me! Huh, giant's racket stopped the bloomin' bird squawkin' though. Right, while it's quiet, I'm gonna tie it up in me shirt. Here, you jeepin' thing, get yer head down here. Oh, no, yer not getting yer neck out the end – I'm gonna tie these sleeves together. Damn you, get yer beak back down there. It'd be easier if I could tie yer on my back, I could climb down then, but how the heck am I going to climb down this tree thing with only one hand and a bolshie bird under me arm? I wish Zack was here, he'd have an idea, a brainwave or something. Huh, can't squawk now and give me away, can you? What'm I going to do, up this giant tree with this here giant smelling me blood?

> "I've sought him here. I've sought him there.
> He dun't seem to be ... nowhere."

Nowhere? I'm right here behind this chair, mate. Chair? Bigger than our whole house! And, more jeepin' bad poetry as well! Crumbs, even I can write better than that.

> "Amelia Jones. Amelia Jones,
> The sight of you makes watery all my bones."

Now there's real poetry for you. Oh Amelia, is there anything about yer I don't love? I love the way yer giggle – I don't always know why yer gigglin', but it's lovely anyway. And yer just love that little mirror I left on yer windersill that night – never knew where that came from, did yer? But I see yer lookin' in it all the time, and I love yer lookin' in it, and, well, I just love yer more and more. Yer know, it's all your fault I'm up here at all, being terrorised by this giant, smellin' me blood. Yer never close the curtains in yer bedroom right to. What's a lad to do if there's a handy tree right outside, and if I hadn't climbed up that tree so much, I wouldn't be good at climbin' and I wouldn't be up here. So there!

Pity about yer dad though. You must know he's a right nutter. I hope it dun't run in families. Me Mam says we're not to – what's the word – aggravate him.

You leave him alone, she says – often! *The poor man is grieving his wife. Grief takes people in different ways, I should know* (dab at her eyes – again). *If he needs to cosset her favourite cow, then just let him be.*

Cosset! Soaping it down every day and putting a coat on it in winter's just plain mad. And I'm mad with love for you, darlin' Amelia.

And what are you going to do about it? Why would a girl as rich and giggly as Amelia look at you, Jack Hiscock? If you want my opinion, you need a plan.

She's got an opinion on everything, my Mam.

> "The search is still on. He can't get away.
> I'll find him sooooon,
> But now … eerm bray? eerm, play? eerm tay?
> Yeah! Today!
> But now, today,
> I'll just sit down and have a snoooooze."

More bad poetry. This bird'd better be laying golden eggs – I've got to get summat out of all this. And me Mam thinks I don't plan, does she? So, just how does she think I get out of doing the chores so often? Does she think I just happen not to be there when there's things to be done? Ok, sometimes I actually, really have to do some of the work. Like today, making it look like I was going to chop wood, I sharpened the axe, didn't I? Then, then! The minute her back was turned, up this tree – now there's planning for you.

Odds on she'll never send me off to market again after I came back with them beans. But that guy was straight up and he did say these beans were magic and, if I do say so meself, I am a pretty good judge of character.

Magic beans? On the market? A straight up guy? How did you get SO daft? Not from my side of the family, that's for sure.

"ZZZZZ
ZZZZZZZZZZZZZZZZZ
ZZZZZZZZZZZZZZZZZZZZZZZZZZ"

Jeeps, that noise. What's he doing? Is that snoring? No, stop, you rotten bird. Shut up! Stop squawkin'. You're not going anywhere. Snoring? Well, I know about snoring! Me Mam just about shakes our house down most nights. She'd give this giant a run for his money in the snoring stakes. But think about that, Jack. When Mam snores slower, that means she's well asleep. So if I wait till this giant snores really slowly, then he'll be fast asleep and I can nip out of here and down home. Yes! A plan. But how am I going to get down this tree? I can't do it one handed.

"Z Z Z Z Z Z Z Z Z Z Z Z Z Z Z Z Z
Z Z Z Z Z Z Z Z Z Z"

That's it, nice giant, that's it, slower and slower – ok, louder and louder as well, but as long as it's slower. Think, Jack, think! One, I've got to keep the goose. Two, I've got to have both hands to climb down. So I need something to tie the goose to me back. But what? Something with two long bits to tie round me, and wide in the middle to keep the goose in place. But ... I've got nothin' with me. Just what I'm standin' up in.

A plan, our Jack. You need a plan.

I'll show you, Mam. I'll get a plan. This time I'll really show you, and Zack and Amelia, the whole lot of you. Think, Jack, think.

*

(with, *in italics*, her thoughts)

"Jack, stop playing silly buggers. Come out now. This's gone on too long."

I won't worry. I won't. But he never misses his grub – he hardly had any breakfast and it's dinnertime now. Still, there's little enough.

"And what's this? Where did this bloomin' great tree come from? It wasn't there yesterday. I'd've noticed. It's got to be summat to do with Jack. I just know it. What are those things hanging from it? Runner beans?"

Oh, giant trees, no Jack, no money, no cow. Where's it all going to end? That cow was the last thing I had. I didn't want to sell it, but what could I do? And now that's gone. Magic beans! And this's a magic beanstalk, I s'pose! I'll bloomin' kill that boy when I get him. His dad was bad enough, but somehow, he'd always pull us through. I never thought it'd be so hard without him. Never thought he'd go so soon. Didn't think about it at all, really. Well, you don't, do you? No, don't get upset again, you've got Jack to look to now. But what can I do? Where can I turn next? Nowhere. Nothing left. If these things are runner beans at least we could live off one of them for a few weeks, but ...

"Mam. Mam. Get the axe."

"Eh? Jack?"

"Mam. The axe!"

"Jack, where are you? What're you up to now?"

"Up here, Mam. Just get the axe. The axe!"

"Up where? Up this tree. God in heaven! Is that you, our Jack? Where's yer trousers? And no underpants! Oh ... God in ... Blimey! What's that lump on yer back? Is them feathers stickin' out yer ... ? No, they're comin' out the lump, not yer ... What're you up to now?"

"Mam, get the axe. I've gorra plan."

"Bloody heck. A plan? You? The axe's right here, where you left it, my lad! You just stand there – I'll tek the bloomin' axe to you!"

"No, tek this goose. I only had me trousers to tie it on with. Quick, give us the axe. Don't let that bird go for God's sake. I'll tell you about it in a minute."

"A goose! A big one an' all. Blimey, this'll keep us going for a good bit. I'll make some pate and sell it to butcher – nah, he's a right tightarse, I'd get more at market. Get the fat. Nice, goose fat, and there'll be a lot on you, me lovely goosey. No, stop squawkin'! Jack, what you doin'?"

"I'm choppin' this tree down. There's a giant chasin' me."

"A giant? And does that amaze me more than the sight of you working? Chopping down a tree? I'll have to get you some underpants. Well, at least we'll be warm in winter with all this wood. You'll need some new trousers; this bird's pecking yours to death."

I didn't know he could work so hard. P'raps I should've taken his trousers off him sooner.

"It's coming, Mam. It's coming."

And standing together, for the first time since they couldn't remember when, Jack stark-bollock naked, his Mam in clothes so old she'd forgotten how ragged they were, together they watched as the tree split, cracked, and started to fall, fall, fall, the top coming out of the clouds, crashing down, landing right over on the other side of the valley, shaking, it seemed, the whole earth, shaking down their own little hut, covering everything in dust and leaves.

*

PART THREE – THIRD PERSON NARRATOR
(with, *in italics,* one thought from Jack)

Well, only fairy stories end with the defeat of the giant. Real life has consequences. When Jack had convinced his

Mam of the golden eggs, and they'd hidden a few away, they had to face the villagers.

People were furious. Houses shattered. Babies screaming. Chickens running around everywhere. It looked like Jack and his Mam'd be run off, probably tarred and feathered as well.

But Jack showed the villagers where the giant's palace had fallen, and how it was full of gold and jewels and giant coins and fabulous fabrics, masses of it, just there for the taking. Bits of the giant were splattered around, but nobody was squeamish. Anyway, faster than you could blink, they changed tune, filled their pockets as full as they could, hoisted Jack and his Mam onto their shoulders and carried them right to the pub. Jack's Mam stood drinks for the whole village, on tick, but the barman didn't bother about that for the moment.

Some people wondered where the butcher had gone – not a man to miss a free drink usually, but they'd soon downed too much to bother and when he turned up with these enormous steaks and started a barbecue, offering them really cheap, well, then everyone just had to have a few more bevvies to celebrate.

Somebody called Jack 'gold bringer' and 'man of gold'. All the villagers took up the chant.

"Gold man, yeah, yeah, yeah. Gold man. Gold man." The pub echoed with it.

Hmm. Goldman. I like that. thought Jack. *Better than Hiscock, anyway.*

And they all had a bit more to drink – well, quite a lot more, actually.

*

But one person was not pleased by all the gold and riches. Farmer Jones, Amelia's dad. His wife's cow had been killed by an enormous skillet, flying out of the giant's kitchen. He was inconsolable. Jack thought his chances with Amelia were pretty slim now, given he'd effectively killed her dead mother's favourite cow.

He'd tried walking over the tree to see Amelia, much quicker than going down dale and up hill, but the branches and twigs tore at his new designer shellsuit, so he came home and had a chat with Zack – Zack was his business manager now – and then paid to have the tree flattened and shaped into a real road with two lanes in each direction for traffic, and wide pavements and turnstiles. They made some of the side branches into observation points with steps so people could climb up them. These were a WOW – people came from all over to look at the view, stand in the observation points and bungee off them. Zack charged more for that; soon he and Jack were coining it in.

News of the wonderful bridge reached the capital city, and the king said he'd like to come and have a look, so Zack arranged a grand opening – charged an arm and a leg for tickets (which sold out in minutes!) – and the king came, with his daughter, the princess.

Jack's Mam looked great. With her hair done, professional make-up – she'd a live-in beauty therapist these days – but mainly with no worries about money, she looked the bee's knees. The king said nice things to her and invited them both for a cup of tea at the palace next time they were in the capital city, and everyone said how nice the princess was, given she was royal, and an orphan and a teenager to boot.

When all the fuss had died down, Jack and his Mam settled into their big new house and the goose into its new goosehouse. Mostly they sat on one of the verandas watching their favourite view of money being made as traffic and people crowded across the tree-bridge.

One day, Jack's Mam was a bit fidgety.

"You know, our Jack,' she said, "I've been thinking. We've caused Farmer Jones a great loss and sadness."

She blushed a bit and carried on.

"P'raps we should pay him, and Amelia, of course, pay

them both a visit, you know, to offer our … um … our condolences. It's a pity for them to be on their own. With their sadness."

Jack took a long drink.

"Mmmm, that's what you've been thinking, is it?"

"Well, yes," she said, going even redder in the face.

Jack paused before he spoke.

"Well, what I've been thinking, is that it gets very cold in this valley in the winter."

"Yeeesss? said Mam, a bit bemused.

"So p'raps, come the cold weather, we should go south for a few weeks. Get a bit of sun. Take in the sights. Go to the capital city. And, of course, it'd be downright rude not to take the king up on his invite for a cuppa with him and … with the princess."

Jack's Mam looked long and hard at him before replying.

"You've got a plan, our Jack, haven't you? A big plan." There was admiration in her voice.

"You know, Mam, I think I have." said Jack. "Yeah." he said more definitely, "Yeah, I have."

He smiled. She smiled. The golden-egg-laying goose stood up, flapped its wings, and squawked long and loud and neither of them told it to shut up.

You Win

Sarah Davy

I am clearing out your flat when I find it. The pink lottery ticket is tucked under a discoloured photo fridge magnet. You and me wrapped in a neon towel on a windswept beach. A picture-perfect father and daughter. I pocket the magnet and move to tear the ticket in half. The ridge of you stops me, your words in heavy biro under my thumb. I lift the printed side to the light of my phone first, then punch the numbers into the app and wait while they tally with the matching draw. One matching number, then three, then six. I re-enter them. Still a match. I read the ticket again, check the date. Six weeks old. I comb through the pile of newspapers for the memory of an article and find the front page of last week's Courant, '*Search for lucky local mystery winner of unclaimed jackpot*'. Clean sweep. Millionaires.

Millionaire.

Shock closes my fist around the ticket. I breathe then smooth it back out, clean the creases with my fingernails. Your handwritten list is on the reverse. There are five instructions. The questions that rattled round my mind after your accident are answered. You were never that unlucky. I fold the ticket in half, then again and tuck it in the hidden pocket of my purse. Close my eyes to the sound of brakes and tyres and your broken body. Conjure you back to life to dance around the kitchen throwing twenty-pound notes into the air. Open my eyes to silence and shadows.

I move upstairs and put the last bin bag on the pile for the council, pull the door shut and push the key back through the letterbox.

1. Post brown parcel.

The first task is simple.

I make a final trip to your lock up. The row of garages is tucked up a lane and flanked by a rattling main line and scrappy woodland. I kneel next to the burned-out car and fish the spare key out of its miraculously intact glove box. A rat bursts out of a pile of bin bags, trailing ribbons of paper behind it. I move to the unit, expecting a fight with the rusted lock, but the key turns smoothly, leaving a film of WD40 on my fingertips. The door glides up and over and I pull it shut behind me. The walls are freshly whitewashed, a bright bulb overhead. A milk crate filled with parcels and envelopes sits alone in the centre of the space. Everything is labelled in thick black marker that fills my head with memories of sniffs and giggles behind textbooks. You laughed when they sent me home from school, checked my pupils then sent me to bed early, and never mentioned it again. I was your golden girl, untroubled by rules and retribution. My mistakes paled in the wake of you and the rivers of muck that ran underneath our feet, upturning us. We bobbed along together in bin lids on torrents, landing now and again only to be chased back out into the storm. Until I couldn't weather it any longer and you sailed off without me. The beginning of your spiral. I bring the roller door down, lock it and throw the key over the lane into a tangle of blackberries and nettles. Only the rat dragging a pizza crust across the cracked tarmac is my witness.

At the post office, the clerk weighs the box. He lifts it carefully, shakes it to make his assessment then asks about its contents. *Just books*, I tell him. Our stock answer. He curls his lip then hands me the slip, which I fold and hide next to the list, the last piece of you. I replay how I imagine the street, the lights, the car and the crushing sounds of that moment. Shocked faces, futile attempts, pieces of you scattered across the tarmac. Sparkles of broken glass and twisted metal. I build a new memory of you instead.

Stepping out, one foot in front of the other. The reservoir never happened and you walk the narrow lanes of your forgotten village and climb the steps to your childhood home. *Accidents happen,* I told myself when they knocked on the door and took off their hats. But never to you. Never to us. There was always a plan.

> 2. *Hand deliver white parcels.*
> 3. *Follow instructions inside grey envelope.*

Two and three take longer. There are long roads to travel in taxis paid in cash, to places I worked hard to forget. But you always found a way of drawing me back, of winding the spool back in. I wade through overgrown front gardens littered with shards of swing sets and climbing frames, knock on boarded up doors and ignore the waft of curtains and hushed voices. The weight of the list starts to pull at my shoulder, nipping my earlobe. Black printed numbers seep through my leather purse, pierce my skin and settle in my veins. There is no instruction for this piece of you, for the puzzle you've left me to solve, that might never be solved. For every secret you whispered in my ear, every plan you let me in on, a thousand more lay unspoken. You kept me safe by keeping me close and far away and now I can only drift along the path you set and hope to wash up somewhere with solid ground underneath my feet.

I shake hands with strangers and pass envelopes stuffed with bank notes through letterboxes, listening first for a snarl of teeth that could tear the money to shreds. The last door is opened by a tiny woman, hair in curlers so large the weight of her head on her slender neck seems impossible. She clears lipstick from her teeth, takes a long draw from her cigarette. A date and time is agreed. We set alarms on phones, repeat instructions until they are tattooed on our eyelids. Nothing is written down. Only your list. Your final adventure is in motion, a journey home planned to perfection by the only person you could trust. You.

4. *Break me the fuck out.*

The storm that always chased us catches up with me. Four begins as you would have wanted. I am head to toe in black with two men whose faces I can't see and am pleased I never will. Windows shatter and a morgue worker is knocked unconscious. The men lift him carefully and tuck him inside a cold, empty casket. Lights flash and alarms ring. We move. I hear doors, then voices travelling towards us but the men push the trolley and tell me to look forward, never back. We arrive outside in a torrent. In the eye of the storm our cargo is loaded carefully and tethered to the floor. I climb up, buckle myself in and the van doors slam shut behind me. In the back of the shelled-out Transit, we are alone together again.

My accomplices can't believe we managed it. They turn up the radio and sing giddy like schoolgirls as we hurtle through the early morning light of the city, squeezing through suburbs until we hit cool open motorway. I curl my fingers around yours, seek out your broad grip but feel only bone and skin. Your last years have drained you. I want to lift the blanket and search for the fire that burned so hard you died to snuff it out. The men tell me not to, that I should remember you as you were. They know what you've been through and what it did to you when I left. I want to squeeze you back to breathing to scream at you and make you cry for disappearing, for choosing, for leaving me alone and letting it end this way. Your stillness and cool quiet is so alien my blood slows. The stone in the pit of my stomach whenever trouble arrived is air, and I am halfway between flying and falling through myself.

*

I didn't count the money for the two men but know it was enough. They are warmer now, sharp edges rounding as they drive, recalling you and the day you carried me into the lockup. *Those eyes*, they say. *God your mother must have been beautiful.* I never met her, the woman who left one night without a goodbye. You told me I was the image of her, and if I ever wanted to see her you stood me in front of the mirror, undid my plait and ran my hair over my right shoulder. You never stayed long but I did, staring into the pool of our eyes.

The main road turns to rough track and we bump for a mile until we reach the perimeter fence that surrounds the reservoir. There is no easy way through. You are lifted over it gently, head-first then feet. I unload wood and rope and fuel, throw piece by piece over the mesh while the men knot and assemble and soak. It is noon when we finish, sweat drenched, muscles burning. We sprawl on the gravel shore and open our flasks. The broader man passes round clingfilmed sandwiches then turns away to lift his balaclava and eat. Ham and pease pudding on white bread with lukewarm sweet tea never tasted as good.

We settle you in place gently on the newly built raft. It is anchored to a lightning scorched sycamore and bobs gently on the shoreline. The men gather their tools and leave, scaling the fence and taking the forest path back to the road and the car you left covered under a thicket of brambles. I'll never see them again, and they'll separate at the services, their last job complete. Both squeezed my shoulder, then leant over you and whispered. Words to sail away on. Things they'd never say while you were breathing.

The sun is still high, hours of August left until nightfall but I need more time. To think, to process, to put the pieces together. To wonder how things got so bad that this was your only escape route. Water seeps through my socks, cool and delicious. I let it pool between my toes. Summer has stolen the lake, the level so low tips of your drowned village appear, a strange horizon. I wonder if the windows survived, want to wade out to scrub glass clear and peer into sitting rooms and kitchens, see life playing out. Kettles boiling, bowls on tables, soup bubbling over. To climb the steps and open your front door and sit with you. But I have one last task. A job to tick off your list.

5. *Send me home.*

Sirens echo down the valley from the main road. Time is running out. Soon, there will be voices. Reasoning. Possibly force. This is number five, the ending you always wanted. My hands shake as I grip the petrol-soaked torch left by the men. A heron unfolds its wings and takes off silently, keeping low to the water until it reaches ridge tiles. The air is completely still and I lift my face to the sun and hold it there until my cheeks turn pink.

Voices push through the thicket of Himalayan balsam. Just a wire fence and the gravel shore between them and us. The anchoring knot undoes easily and you bob free from the sycamore, the gentle motion of the water holding you close. It will take all my strength to push you out. I take a long, full breath, flick the lighter and hold it to the torch. Nothing. I try again, fight the tremble coursing through me. *Steady,* you would say, *quiet yourself.* But I have nothing left. The torch slips from my hand and is swallowed by the slick cool of the reservoir. Feet on gravel behind me. I need paper, card, something to tuck under your shroud. Then I feel it. The tendrils that set root, black printed numbers trickling through my veins. The final piece. Everything you'd ever wanted, more money than sense, a way out after a lifetime of running, hiding, sweating in the dark while people rattled windows. A solution. Your solution. Not mine.

When we watched films together you floated away. Into romance, into longing, into fantasy. I never believed in fairy-tale endings, in getting what you want. You made sure of that, even if you didn't mean to. I fish my purse from my pocket and unfold the lottery ticket. It lights first time. I hold it to the bracken lined raft and push you out into the water. Your embers fizz and crackle then roar and the vessel comes alive. I am waist deep watching you leave when a hand gently squeezes my shoulder and closes cool metal cuffs over my wrist.

Meeting Others Safely Outdoors

Monica Dickson

The National Trust car park has plenty of spaces. Dave and his family are early. They are always early. Dave is worried he has told the other two families the wrong car park. Dave is a worrier. Dave's surname is Bravery, which is unfortunate.

The other two families arrive in the car park. Dave has not told them the wrong car park; he has told them the right one. Dave knows he needs to stop worrying. You die if you worry and you die if you don't, Dave's mum used to say. Dave's mum is dead now, so she should know.

The children are all on their phones. It is hard to get the children out of the car when they are on their phones. Dave's wife, Claire Bravery, tells their son, Alfie, to get out of the car. Claire says it nicely because the other two families, the Nixons and the Grants, are within earshot. The Nixons and the Grants ask their children to get out of the car nicely too. The sun is shining and everyone is being nice to each other.

The Nixons, the Grants and the Braverys are going on a walk today. They have not seen each other, in person, since dinner parties and playdates became illegal. Dave has planned the walk. It is a new walk. Dave has a map. Dave's friends are making fun of him.

Dave will get us lost, says Kev Nixon.

Dave is going to tell us where to go, says Zane Grant.

Zane is still irked about the last time the Grants and the Braverys went on a walk together. The last time the Grants and the Braverys went on a walk together was a long time ago, before Alfie Bravery was born and Dave decided it was a good idea to walk up a big hill. Zane and Sally's son, Finn, was too big to be carried and too little to walk up a big hill. But Sally Grant really, really wanted to walk up a big hill because Sally had been stuck at home with little Finn for a very long time. So, Zane stayed at the bottom of the hill, with little Finn, who sat in his buggy and cried for two hours straight. Zane blamed Dave. Dave blamed Sally. Nobody is sure whose fault it was.

Ten years on, all the children can walk by themselves. They are big boys and girls. The mums miss holding their hands, but they do not miss having to walk very slowly and stop every few seconds to look at another leaf. Mel Nixon is mum to twins, Hattie and William. Hattie and William are eleven years old. Hattie and William are always up to mischief. Today, Hattie is bending William's fingers backwards until he screams. Kev says Mel is spoiling them rotten. Mel smiles a big, bright smile and says she has just given up trying to get them to do as they are told, which is different.

The families chat as they put on their walking boots. It was a long drive. The traffic was bad. The Grants missed the turn off. The Nixons got flashed. Alfie says he has forgotten to bring his walking boots. He is going to have to wear his wellingtons. Dave picks Alfie up in a fireman's lift, which makes everyone laugh because Alfie is nearly nine and very big boned and now his face is red, like the wellies. Dave laughs the loudest, even though he told Alfie to put his walking boots in the car at least three bloody times.

The families set off on their walk. They start on a very big hill. Claire Bravery and Mel Nixon chat about working from home and homeschooling and tell each other how well they are doing. Sally Grant stays quiet. When there is a lull in conversation the mums call out to their kids.

Hurry up, slow coach, says Claire to Alfie.

Stop punching your brother, Hattie, says Mel.

Don't get too close to the others, Ida, says Sally to Finn's little sister.

The children ignore them.

When they get to the top, Dave is out of breath. He bends to rest his hands on his knees. Dave tells his friends he's in poor shape, now that he's at home all day with nothing to do. Something will turn up old chap, says Zane and pats Dave on the back, even though they are not supposed to touch each other.

The waterfall at the top of the hill is stunning. The families take photos and videos. Hattie is sulking because she has mud on her white jeans.

These are my favourites! she wails.

I told you not to wear the damn things, says Mel but Hattie can't hear her because the waterfall is very noisy. Mel wonders what it would be like to wade through the water and stand underneath the waterfall in all her clothes.

The families keep walking. After twenty minutes Dave realises they have taken a wrong turn. Dave is peeved that Kev and Zane were right about his navigation skills, but he does not want his friends to know that. Instead of getting cross, Dave makes fun of Alfie and the way he walks in his wellies. Alfie ignores him. He is glad he wore wellies because it is very muddy. Stuff you, Dad! thinks Alfie.

Back on track, the families come to a hamlet. They walk through the hamlet and past a farm. The door to the farmer's cottage is open. Out runs a dog. Ida loves dogs. The dog loves Ida. It follows her over a stile into the next field.

The children are getting tired.

I'm starving, says Finn.

Don't say that when there are people in the world who really are starving, says Sally.

People are starving round the corner from where we live, says Claire.

Lunch o'clock! says Mel.

The families throw down blankets. They sit and start to unpack their picnics. Sally has remembered to bring hand sanitizer. Everyone agrees that Sally is very organised.

Mel has a brain like a sieve, says Kev.

You pack the sodding bag next time then, Kev, says Mel. Mel does not care that everyone can hear.

The families eat their lunches. The sun has gone in. It

is starting to rain. Hattie and Ida huddle together with the farmer's dog. Somewhere between the car park and the farm they have forgotten about government social distancing guidelines. No one can remember if they are allowed to share food either. They think it is probably okay if it came from a reputable shop and the grown-ups agree that Waitrose All Butter Flapjack Bites are just the thing to keep everyone going.

Alfie has finished his lunch and is standing on his own, kicking a rock. Since he stopped going to school, Alfie wakes up in the night, so he is very tired and grumpy. So are Dave and Claire. Dave and Claire haven't had sex in six months. Dave thinks they need relationship therapy. Claire thinks they just need to be away from Alfie for more than a few minutes at a time. The couples talk about what they've been binge-watching. Sally Grant laughs at one of Kev Nixon's jokes. Kev tries not to look too pleased with himself. Global events have put Kev and Sally's affair abruptly on pause and clandestine Skype calls are not quite the same.

The children are getting restless. Hattie and Ida have stopped petting the dog. They have put on their face coverings and are playing a game of Am I Smiling Or Am I Not Smiling? Everyone laughs. Except for William and Finn. William and Finn are arguing about Minecraft. Last night, William put lava in Finn's nether fortress and Finn is having a hard time forgiving him. Vengeance will be mine, yells Finn. The mums and dads all agree that Minecraft is very educational, though none of them are sure how, exactly.

The families set off again. Dave leads the way and everyone follows. They have walked through three more fields before they notice that the farmer's dog is also following. Dave is worried that the farmer's dog will get lost. Claire checks its collar. She calls the phone number on the dog's ID tag. Dave and Claire turn back, with the dog, towards the farm, leaving Alfie with the other families.

How much longer? My wellies are rubbing, cries Alfie.

Nobody is sure how much longer because Dave has gone off with the map. They follow the sign saying public footpath and push on up the next big hill.

Mel is telling Sally about her new job. She has only met her colleagues online so far, but they've invited her to attend a fundraising event. Mel is not sure how many people will be there but thinks it will be alright to go if it's for charity. Mel asks Sally how she is. Sally was staying at home long before it became compulsory. She calls herself a 'full time mum', which annoys Mel, but they are friends all the same.

Sally tells Mel she is fine. Did she mention Finn has been hitting himself in the face with the Xbox controller? Oh, and Ida has pulled out all her eyelashes. Sally starts to cry and Mel is not allowed to hug her.

Fucking hell, Sally, says Mel, which works just as well.

Up ahead, Kev, Zane and the children have stopped walking. A herd of cows is blocking the gate to the next field. The children are not sure what to do. Kev and Zane are not sure what to do. Kev says it reminds him of a school trip to Peru, when they came across a herd of llamas.

Aren't llamas just goats with long necks, Dad? asks William.

Shut up, William, says Kev.

Yeah shut up, William, you idiot, says Harriet.

While Kev tries to break up the fight, Zane walks towards the cows. Zane waves his arms and makes a funny noise. He tells the children the worst thing you can do is run. The cows start to move. The children start to run.

Once they are safely at the other end of the field, the families stop. Claire and Dave are catching up with them. Claire looks worried. Dave looks the colour of a dry stone wall.

Wait for us, pants Dave. Dave does not feel well. It was a long walk back to the farm. Alfie runs towards his dad and Dave stumbles. Dave lowers himself to the ground.

He is sweating. Dave waves the map. Claire takes the map. They are still twenty minutes from the car park.

I don't think Dave's going to make it, says Claire.

*

The weekly Zoom quiz starts at two. Sally is in the kitchen making almond butter hummus. Mel is in the hot tub drinking Porn Star Martinis. Kev is in his study, texting Sally from under the desk. Zane is hosting. Zane has forgotten to compile the questions, what with all the fuss and bother on their walk yesterday. The families wait for Zane to look up general knowledge quiz questions that they haven't already had. Ida yawns. Hattie pouts. William scowls. Finn beams. Finn has hidden monster spawn in William's underground bunker: vengeance is his.

Alfie sits behind Claire, playing with his Lego. He doesn't notice when Dave appears on screen. Dave has dialled in from his hospital bed. Claire hasn't seen him since yesterday, when the farmer turned up on his quad bike and drove Dave to the nearest A&E. The doctors tell Dave it's a panic attack. They are keeping him in for further assessment.

You die if you worry and you die if you don't, Dave tells the psychiatrist, tugging at the collar of his hospital gown.

Isn't Dave lucky it's all in his head? says Claire.

Sally nods.

Mel claps.

Zane and Kev give a thumbs up.

Dave tries to get Alfie's attention.

Son, mouths Dave, waving, leaning in towards the camera. Son!

You're on mute Dave, says Claire. You need to take yourself off mute.

Fragments of Stone

Lydia Gill

You hated birthdays. You paced. And cleaned the skin of fruit. Cloth dipped in water. One part bleach. Peaches were for special occasions. Fuzz burnt away.

Bin bags were a comfort on birthdays. The sleek of them through your hands. Their dark openings. How they captured air.

You did not take visitors. Not even once a year. They brought things inside. Offerings. Dirt.

It was the wrapping paper. About birthdays. And Christmas was worse. New items needing boxing. Leftovers.

A vase on a shelf looks wrong.

I look out of the window. John Alan is working on a gravestone.

Never put flowers on my grave, you said. They'll only go to mush.

There's a series of empty fields. A beck running through. A silver seam. The sight of the stone yard. But the drystone walls aren't symmetrical. That might have nagged at you. Ha ha. I test a laugh. It falls onto the carpet. Ha ha. Ha. Laughter falls like a piece of chiffon. Flattens onto the floor.

Even laughter was frivolous. Frilled. It floated through the house. And tore. Chiffon was not for you. It was for women in pubs. On corners.

There is nothing to sort out anyway. There are outlines where things used to be. Patches of paint untouched by sunlight. A smell of bleach that sharpens the emptiness.

*

The town is thriving with pubs. People vape. Plumes of menthol lift into grey. An outskirt supermarket squats on the horizon. Shop shutters are lazy eyes. Laziness is the disease of our time, you said. Charity shops jostle. Racks of clothes are left to the street. Women finger dresses. Their faces creased into frowns. At the St Jude Hospice Shop the door buzzes. Someone scuffles out back. With you in a minute! The voice is scraped by something. Cigarettes. Lung disease.

Here the shelves heave up flowered crockery and porcelain figurines shine with curves that I want to skim with my fingertips and I could flick at every trinket that hangs from a rack and books splay their pages open and piles of scarves entwine like arms in baskets and there's twisted strap handbags and squished flat hats and all manner of fussy bits fuss fussiness and even the lampshade has tassels like hair and the volunteer lady comes out of the back she is scrawled with tattoos and a scuff of grey cuts her dye job in two and she smiles up a smudged lip and says, that a birthday badge, and I say, yeah yeah work made me wear it, and it's a lie and she tells me, hang on wait there a minute, and brings out a photo in a plain silver frame and says, looks like you this does, and it is me and I realise the photo was dumped here like everything else and that seems like enough for today doesn't

*

There were nits. Little sharp combs to lift them. Eye-burning lotions. It'll have to come off you said. All of it? All of it. Can't have it.

Who the fuck you think you are lad? He said when I walked in. Sinead Fucking O'Connor? She off on one? Mad bloody cow. Time I speak to the social. Again. Here have some crisps. He pinched his cigarette out. The ash tray overflowed. Bullseye came on. You better get home birdman. See you next Sunday.

John Alan is carving a name. His arms are smooth with dust. The vase has had time to settle on the shelf. A shadow has slipped behind it.

A woman trips out of a pub. A smile sharpens at the corner of her mouth. Oopsy, she says. Don't s'pose you got a spare smoke? Sorry, no, I don't. She has drawn on her eyebrows. Lots of tiny brushstrokes. Her face is blanked with foundation. There's a slick of grease at the puff of her lips. Shame, she says swaying. Baltic out here though. What time is it please? Four thirty, I say. Sorry I have to I have to go. Shops'll shut soon. See you then, she replies. And shivers. A quick pull of breath.

At the St Jude Hospice Shop the door buzzes and catches on the lino. The buzz goes on. Give it a shove! says the woman's rough voice.

And the trousers press together in a fleshy kind of way like scissoring legs and all the little plastic toys are scattered on the floor so a kid has been in and the curtain of the changing room bulges and flits while someone breathes behind it and, sorry about the other day, says the volunteer lady, I didn't think at all, and I ask her, did she come in here to drop that photo off? And the woman says, she, and then she says, no it was dumped out front in a shoe box I think we're still tagging it up you can come out back if you like and have a look through, and I think of out back and the mounds of the bags and I start to swell and split open, no I don't have time today but if could you put it aside for me, I say, my body turned away so that she can't see how

I locked my room once. Imagined things piled under beds. What would you be doing in there then Rob? You called. Moving past on your slippered feet. Don't fret I called out. Nowhere to hide pornos. The words fell out. You heard them. You're not too old for a good bath you said, cold. Your stare passing through the door. Your fingers flexed on the handle. Strong from cleaning. I was sure you could still take the scruff of me. Plonk me into scalding water. Rub me into pink. Into the thin swirl of blood that runs from a chafing.

The brittle loofah. A skeletal thing. I would look into its intricacy. Its depth. Find the darkest of its inner places. Its cells were minute twists of bone. Each one a tiny place to contain something. Something small enough to fit. Curled up and crouched. I would find those places. While you rasped the dirt off me.

I unlocked the door. The next day the lock was gone. Four holes left in the wood.

*

There is a snowdrop. I took it from John Alan's place. It was easier than I thought. Adding one thing to another. A snowdrop. In a vase. On a shelf.

*

There's a market on. It's Thursday. I turn round and go home.

*

Are you Robin Harland? she asked. A policewoman stood on the doorstep. Her hat in her hands. You stopped calling me Robin. At some point I became Rob. Another rubbing out. A policeman hovered behind her. He looked hard into the street. Didn't meet my eye. Mind if we come in? What is what's it all about this? I asked her. I knew though. It would be better if we came in. She looked at the bin bags behind me. Don't run, she shouted. Don't run.

John Alan is finishing the gravestone. He paints into the letters with black. A long brush. Certain strokes. He steps back from time to time. No room for error. Imagine starting that again. There are blocks of stacked stones. They lean up against a wall. Each one waits to be marked.

The snowdrop has wilted. Stained with age. I'm relieved. I have let it go. So far.

You should have been a dentist. In another life. Buffing.
Extracting. The wipe clean chair.

A white overcoat.

No fillings today. Just like every other time. You're my
worst customer, the dentist says. What do you clean them
with? Bleach, I say. Aha, he laughs. I'll let my other pa-
tients know. But then they might stop having them whit-
ened. True. The dentist is at the end of the high street.

At the St Jude Hospice Shop they have mended the door.
It slides smoothly over the lino.

Oh God it is sorting day and bin bags spill onto the shop
floor exposing their stuffing their guts of leggings and coils
of sleeves and shoes flap like dead fish and the volunteer
lady is squatting beside them and there's a stamp of a lotus
in a triangle of back flesh and hiya, she says, with a sad
sorry smile, look I kept things aside that were left out back
just like you asked me to there wasn't much I'm afraid just
a shoe box of stuff do you want to take it home with you
not paying for it I mean, and she presses the box that sags
in the centre into my hands and she smells like incense and
her fingers are dry but to know someone like her would be

I let the thought rest like a stone in a hand.

*

Fuck's happened? You look white as a sheet, he said.
It's her isn't it. She tried it again? I'll get on the phone.
It'll have to be police this time, Birdman. How was she
when you left? Breathing? Ambulance then. They'll take
her away. Maybes leave the police out of it. You're old
enough now lad. Live on your own.

I looked around the room. The TV singed the air with
light. A thin line of smoke rose from the ash tray. Unbroken
by movement. And it seemed to be a sign. I could stay
here, I said. No lad, love. You know what Sheila said. Not

after last time. You know where I am though. Let's keep up the Sundays. Ambulance please.

*

The shoe box is quite full. I expected more space. A pair of reading glasses in a red case. A cloth for cleaning them. The photo of me. A box of lead pencils. Three gone. A black marker pen. A fragment of stone.

A fragment of stone that's strange that's

And a book. The book draws attention to itself. The cover is gone. Torn off. Pages are foxed at the edges. There's a pen mark straight through the title.

And inside are lines of black. Crossing out every sentence. Every paragraph. Every page.

More bags you said. Out back. Take them when you go up town on Saturday. What's in them? I asked. Never mind. Is any of it mine? Nothing is yours I pay for it all. I started to open a bag. Don't you dare, you said. You ran at me. Bottle of bleach in hand. It squirted across the corridor. Splattering the carpet. My clothes. My face. See what you've done, you said. That won't come out. Don't rub it with your hands. It's in my bloody my eye, I said. You hissed, get out and take that language with you.

The sky was a painful blue. I was surprised by the warmth. John Alan was in his yard. He looked at me. And started up his stone cutter.

I open and close the book. Flick the pages quickly. The black lines move. Walk across the pages. An optical illusion.

I try to find a mistake. There are none. I think of you sitting on floorboards. The concentration required. The page numbers are left alone. There's a cleanliness to numbers I suppose. The way they obey.

You switched the light on and off three times. When you left a room. Me sat in darkness.

A fragment of stone.

Saturdays were different. Town days. Bin bags in hand. I'd drop them off first. At a charity shop. I don't go into town you said. Not there. Mucky.

I'd often be seen. That your shopping Robin? Ro-bin man. Bin man. No wonder you fucking stink. I knew what they said was untrue. You wouldn't have stood for a smell.

Then I was free. I would start in the car park. Trace round it with my eyes. Pick up each car and put it down again. Take one I liked. Hold it in my hand. With my eyes. Run it round the road. A red one. A blue one. Sometimes a truck. But only with my eyes.

I visited the market. Holding his hand with my lungs. Shall we choose this one or that? Apple or banana? That one, I would point. With my eyes. We'll take both, he would say. And a punnet of cherries. It was hard to hold onto his voice. My head would ache. I'd have to sit down. Count a scatter of chips. He was a pleasant smell. Something soft. Something strong.

He was next to my elbow and he was nowhere at all and he was nothing not real he only lived in that place which pressed on my breath like a hard and swollen pocket of air he could fill it up nicely and stopper all that pressure just for an hour or so I knew that really but

I'd take something. Something that could fit into a pocket. Sometimes a badge. A sweet if I could. Snatched from a pick n mix. One time a liquorice pipe. It bulged in my pocket. I ate it on our doorstep. Realising my mistake. Inside the hoover droned. And I knew what sound it made. The sound of despair. Going on. And on.

*

The book is thick. The page edges greased with turning. I flick them. Smell the breath of the book. I have put on your glasses. Let them rest on my head. Something flashes like a spark. What is it? I flick the pages again. Slower this time. There. A word. I pounce on it with my finger. It's on page forty-nine. Written in pencil.

CLEAVAGE.

There is a sudden grip of hundreds of hooks into my skin like the Velcro of the shoes that had to be polished and shined and dipped in disinfectant and I smack the book shut and think what the fuck and drop it on the floor and what the fuck again and the spidering letters were pencilly thin and shook like sweating fingers would and the thought of you doing that I can't even talk to you now because words are like chalk in my mouth and I lean my face on a window and march up and down and I kick the book under the bed and I can't tidy away that word so easily can I and I spit out the window and I spit and I spit and there is John Alan staring up at me and he

We only had one holiday. From what I can remember. We went to Wales to a place called Borth. The name sounded tidy. We stayed in a caravan. When we arrived you opened your bleach. Can't be too sure, you said. But by the end of the stay I had sand in my toes. It was the sea, you said. It was relaxing, you told me. And you'd watch it intently. The way it rested like metal. How it washed the stones away.

John Alan is cutting a new slab. The diamond blade roars.

We met an old man on the street. In Borth. He stopped still when he saw you. This is your Ted, you said in a murmur. I didn't understand. I didn't know any Ted. He began to speak quickly. It must have been Welsh. Some words were like choking. You replied in English. I have to go now. He put out his hand. He said your name. But it was different. It had shape. Texture. Who was that Ted man? I asked. Not Ted, you said. Taid. Grandfather.

*

It's Thursday. Market day. I press my nail into my palm. See a small carved arch in my skin.

The air is thick with the smell of grease from the pie stall and flesh from the meat stall and two for a pound, someone calls, and four for a fiver and I have to walk sideways to push through the crowd and still they rub up to me the bodies the fingers the thin little carrier bags that bulge with their fruit and the hard shining watermelon and the round bulging plums show the whole lot is growing and ripening into being and it's not far to go but soon I will loosen and spill over and I can't let it happen if it does then

The door is propped open at the St Jude Hospice Shop. The angle is a relief. The shadow it cuts so definite.

I am the only customer. Alone today? I ask. Yeah, says the volunteer lady. And I know. And I take her into my hands and the parts of her are soft. And hard. Like things contained in a plastic bag.

A fragment of stone.

*

The snowdrop is dead. Spilled over. Shrivelled to brown. To a twist.

The book is flayed. Cover gone. Why did you do that? I am sick with myself. But I pick it up. A punishment I suppose. I flick the pages fast. Hope I won't see it. But there it is. A minute change in pattern. Appears like a ghost. Back I go. Flick. There. I bookmark it with my thumb. Page one hundred and four.

BACK BUTTERING.

I hate what you have done you have ruined it all and if there was only one thing I could be sure of it was your spotless your spotlessness how your mind was like the marble that statues are carved out of and I am running out of breath for you and I lie on the carpet and watch how the curtain flickers the light and how dust lines the windowsill and everything

Slows. Down.

Dead? I say. Yeah, she says. I'm sorry. Is there someone I can call? There's no. No. There's no one, I say. She pats my knee. Don't touch me, I think.

Sorry about before, I say. I knew what you were going to tell me. I suppose. I didn't want to hear it.

People do funny things, says the policeman. When we turn up at the door.

Three days you said? That's what they think yeah, she replies. It was natural causes they say. From the you know.

Three days. I wonder. What does three days do? What mess. What stains. How indelible.

I lean back into the wall. Try to fit into the shape of the absent chair. Become the blank paint.

*

There's a new pencilled word in the book.

KERF.

I don't want to understand it at all it sounds worse than the others and I could try to find out but what would be the

A fragment of stone.

John Alan is carving your name. His teeth are set with his powerful will. I'll go round on Sunday. As usual.

*

You didn't want flowers on your grave.

John Alan agrees. Just us two lads, he says. Looking around the empty crem. There is a tidiness in that. It's fitting.

There's something I don't get. You didn't go into town. But the shoe box was left. Nonetheless.

At John Alan's house the TV is on. The photo of Sheila reflects a gameshow.

Can you teach me it? I ask. The stone cutting.

He stares into the TV. His hand shakes the smoke from the cigarette. Not sure you should be using a saw he says.

I'm better now.

Are you?

Yeah.

He gets up from the sofa. Hands on knees. Back creaking open. He pulls a book from the shelf. Here, he says. Take this. Learn something. It's a book. A thick one. The pages well-turned. *Fragments of Stone. Memoirs of a Stone Mason.*

I never read it. I only looked in the glossary. Admired the words. The way my mouth carved the air. Cut out. Replaced.

ARCHITRAVE.

VEIN CUT.

I've put a new flower in the vase now. I took it from the crem.

OFF FALL. That was my favourite. A remnant. A fragment. From a cut slab.

*

Your old room is coming alive. As I flick on the light. I see the new things. A tasselled lampshade. A photo. An incense holder.

And off again. Outlines in the dark.

And on again. The shadow that is bonded to the vase.

And off again. Some light comes through the curtain gap. Trapped inside are a million specks of dust.

On again.

Incense curling.

Off again.

Dead skin.

On.

Moving.

On.

Breaking apart.

Woven Together in the Depths of the Earth

C S Mee

They finish their tea in silence. Lucy shunts crumbs around the tablecloth and glances out of the window at the empty bird feeders. Phil takes out his phone.

'Shall we go and have a look?' She moves to stand, pushing away the carcass of her scone.

He looks up from his screen. 'You haven't finished.'

'I'm not hungry. Do you want it?'

He shakes his head.

'It's a bit dry.' She pushes the plate further away, trying to disown it, disown the waste of leaving it.

He stands and slips the phone into his back pocket.

'Right,' he says, as though girding himself. 'Let's get on with this.'

Lucy follows him to the entrance, biting her lip. Phil holds the door, and she steps out into the cold where the plants are laid in rows, between stacks of glazed pots and scattered gnomes and fairies.

She dithers. He glances around and snorts.

'We can just have a look,' she suggests. 'Let's see what they've got. We don't have to buy anything if we can't find anything nice. Suitable.'

He pokes at the gravel with the toe of his shoe. 'It's your choice.'

'It's for both of us,' she wants to say. It was always for both of them. She wanted him with her today, needed him with her, but now she wishes that she'd come alone. The irritation flows from him and knocks her back.

She starts down a row of climbers.

There was so much blood. More than she'd expected. So much blood even though it was still early.

'It'll be just like a heavy period,' the doctor had said,

73

stating cold facts with a look meant to convey sympathy.

It wasn't like a heavy period. It was so much more, so much worse. How could he have known?

So much blood, flooding her knickers and soaking her skirt. She had to change twice and then she just sat on the toilet and let it drip.

It had started small, a few days before, a trace on the toilet paper. At first, she hoped they could do something about it. She thought it would stop and the doctor suggested it might. She hoped this was normal, something that happens to many women at this stage.

It is normal enough to happen to many women. That was one thing that surprised her. The colleagues and friends who put a hand on her arm and shared their own stories.

'It was very early,' she tried to say, except it wasn't. It wasn't early when they'd been trying for a whole year. A year of cycles and they were on the point of making appointments to discuss likely problems and tests and treatments. Then it had happened all on its own.

For the first time, the familiar ache didn't herald her period but two lines on a pee stick. Two lines and she'd blinked and blinked and didn't believe it even though inside her she knew it was true. She'd known it was true even before she bothered with the pee stick, but it gave her something to show Phil. Something real. Two lines. This is it.

The joy on his face. The disbelief.

'Can you do another? To be sure?'

Two lines again. They'd danced around the kitchen. Phil had spilled his coffee and mopped it up laughing. Then they'd left for work, late and grinning.

She hugs her coat around her and trudges along the muddy path between palettes of potting soil and trays of infant perennials. At this time of year there's little colour, apart from gaudy blocks of primroses and pansies. Scant shoots, a green tuft or a bare stick poke from most of the pots, their labels promising implausible future blooms.

She was sent for a scan. No heartbeat. No wriggling foetus. Just an empty egg sac. A broken shell, she'd thought. Spilled yoke. The egg sac came later, in a flood of blood, but by then she'd lost hope.

She'd dreaded morning sickness and the pain of labour, hoarding tales of complications and trauma. Now she wonders if she'll ever know the discomfort of pregnancy and childbirth. Will she ever hold a baby of her own, born at term, ripe and kicking? The question rings again and again and she can't shake free of its echoes.

They pass hanging baskets planted with spring flowers, rolls of cracking turf, tubs of lupins, climbers hitched to poles. She's lost among shrubs with unfamiliar names. She turns to Phil, but he's frowning at a seated buddha.

On another day, he'd joke about the leering gnomes and pouting flower fairies. On another day, she'd stagger back to the car bent double with laughter, proud of the looks from middle-aged couples who had nothing to say to each other anymore. Today Phil is silent. Other shoppers pass them, pushing flatbed trolleys laden with pots that seem carefully and knowingly chosen.

She doesn't know what she's looking for. She doesn't know how to look. Their garden was planted by the previous owners of the house. She and Phil have done little but mow the lawn and pull a few weeds. She keeps thinking they should learn to maintain it, to cultivate it for themselves. Study the names of plants and flowers. Read care instructions. Learn to prune and nurture new growth.

She knows there's no use looking for a reason. She knows it wasn't her fault. She knows she followed all the instructions and obeyed all the advice. She knows all of this, but sometimes she doesn't believe it.

It was early, but she'd known she was pregnant for a whole month. A month of cradling her tummy with her hand and her heart. A month of secret smiles and reading. Picturing cells dividing.

After she'd sat dripping on the toilet for a while, she went to wipe herself and there it was on the tissue, she was certain. This dark bubble of blood was no clot. It matched the textbook image of an eight-week foetus. She held it in her trembling hand and recognised the eye in its head and the tail, the beginnings of arms and legs. The end of arms and legs.

She set the tissue down and sobbed.

Later, she wrapped the dark bubble carefully and when Phil came home, they buried it in the garden.

'I couldn't just flush it down the toilet.'

He dug a hole in the empty plot by the lavender and they laid the tiny parcel in the earth. It was like planting a broken seed.

Afterwards she'd looked out of the kitchen window at the dark square of soil and thought it was bare and cold.

'It needs something...' she muttered. 'A little... something to mark it.'

'Mmmn.' She'd taken his grunt for agreement.

That evening she drank a glass of wine for the first time in months and it made her heavy and floating at the same time, then left her with a sharp headache.

She was terribly tired. She called in sick again the following day and slept.

Her body took longer to recover than she'd expected. Phil was concerned, attentive, but they talked little. Perhaps they talked too little.

Lucy had called him at work, her voice knotted with tears so he couldn't understand her at first. He'd retreated to the stationery cupboard for some privacy and listened to her with his eyes fixed on a box of highlighter pens. The brand name 'niceday' stamped his memory of that conversation with cruel irony.

Afterwards he attended a planning meeting and sat

through a twenty-minute presentation on schedule up-dates and forward projections without understanding a word. He kept catching at a statistic or a bullet point, but then he was back in the claustrophobia of the stationery cupboard with its smells of paper and ink and Lucy's sobs through the static of the phone line. Niceday.

He'd gone for a walk at lunchtime, hoping to disentan-gle the confusion of this loss without a loss. An end with no beginning. Two lines on a pregnancy test was all he had to hold. Everything else was buried inside Lucy, inside her body, inside her heart. It was a mystery he'd been waiting to solve and now it was over before he had a chance to hold it for himself.

He hadn't told his colleagues about the pregnancy, so he didn't tell them about the miscarriage. In the afternoon they were impatient with his lack of concentration and dropped sarcastic lines about lunchtime drinking. He wanted to be home with Lucy, but he didn't know how to respond, how to contain this strange grief and not know-ing frustrated him.

He was relieved that she'd wrapped it in tissue. He didn't want to look. They buried it in the garden, beside the lavender. As they stood in the kitchen looking out at the bare plot, Lucy talked about marking the spot and he pictured a tiny tombstone or a weeping angel. It was too much. How do you remember an end with no beginning?

In the following days Lucy remained curled in on her-self. To his surprise, he envied her physical sickness, how her body marked its loss. It was still her secret.

She recognises the roses before she sees their names. They are naked and thorny, a few sharp twigs in a pot, but their labels promise quilted cups of ruby, cream, peach and gold. She hovers over the stumps, turning leaves and la-bels, reading planting instructions without reading them. Is the plot north facing or south facing? Does it matter?

New Dawn. Compassion. The rose names embarrass

her, but she's drawn to the photographs. Could they nurture these bare sticks into soft scented flowers?

Phil has his phone out again. She wants him to look at the roses. She picks a Pink Bliss and lifts the pot. It's heavy with damp soil.

'How about this one?' she turns to him.

He frowns at the thorny stump.

'To plant in the plot.' She sets the pot down and examines a Tranquillity with golden petals. 'Perhaps this is a better colour.'

'A rose?' He's surprised.

'I thought it would be nice. Appropriate.'

'You want to plant a rose?' His face is suddenly light and open.

'I thought we agreed... As a, as a memorial,' she mumbles the word. It's too solemn, too formal, too post-war.

'I thought you wanted one of those fairy things.' He waves in the direction of the gnomes.

'A flower fairy?'

'When you said memorial. I thought you wanted, I don't know, a garden sculpture.'

She looks over at the fairies, with their petal skirts and smirking faces and she wonders if she and Phil know each other at all, even after all this time.

Phil has put his phone away and is inspecting Tranquillities, comparing leaves and shape.

'This is perfect.' He lifts a pot, smiling for the first time that day.

She wants to plant the rose as soon as they're home, but Phil disappears into the shed and spends a long time sorting through rusted tools, shifting old pots and shuffling bags of soil.

'Pass me a spade,' she calls to him.

'I'm just tidying up in here.' Comes his muffled reply. 'They left so much stuff. We should clear it out, most of it's good for the bin.'

He emerges with a spade and comes over to the bare plot. She's placed the rose in the centre.

He frowns at it and then moves the pot forwards and back, searching for the ideal position. 'Perhaps more to this side.' He moves it so far to the left it's almost on top of the lavender.

She watches him for a moment before she understands.

'I think you can dig here,' she says, replacing the rose slightly right of centre. 'If you dig down there you won't... you won't find anything.'

'Right.' He doesn't meet her eyes.

When he starts to dig the hole, she can't stay to watch. She mutters about making tea and goes into the house.

Later, she comes back out with two mugs. Phil is tucking the rose into its bed, patting down the soil around its thorny stem. He straightens up and wipes the dirt from his hands.

'Thank you.' He takes the mug of tea. 'It'll be beautiful.' He's smiling and relaxed.

'If it ever flowers.'

'Of course it will. And it's a much better choice than a flower fairy or a gnome.'

She laughs now. 'Where did you get that idea?'

He shrugs. 'I'm sure you mentioned a sculpture.'

'Why didn't you say anything?'

'I didn't dare, you were so determined. And it was your...' He hesitates. 'It was for you to choose.'

'But it was always...' She starts and then stops. They need to have this conversation, but not now.

The rose label is stuck in the empty pot and she picks it out to keep. *Flowers May to July*. She turns it over to admire the promised golden blooms and finds the dirt-smeared picture showing deep red flowers instead.

She's shocked. 'This is the wrong rose.'

'It's not the one you chose?'

'No. I wanted Tranquillity. The one with golden flowers. I didn't want red.' Blood red. It's too much.

'You didn't mean to get Growing Hope? I thought it was just right.'

'Growing Hope? That's as cheesy as a flower fairy.' She folds her arms, disappointed.

'We must have picked up the wrong pot.' He takes the label. 'It is a striking colour.'

Tears prickle her eyes. She blinks them away.

Phil looks down at the firmly planted rose. 'I'll dig it up and we'll go back for the other one.'

She follows his gaze and thinks how carefully he's set the rose in its plot. She blinks again. She's tired of crying.

'No,' she says. 'Let's not dig up hope.'

He puts his arm around her shoulders, and she leans into him. 'Are we growing hope then?' he asks.

She can hear him smile.

'Maybe,' she sighs. 'If it ever flowers.'

Segments

S K Perry

I stand in front of the greenscreen. The wall opposite shows me myself, underwater. A shark approaches from behind and a small actor in the corner of the video instructs me to mime breast stroke and panic. I wonder how much they got paid and if they'd always dreamed of three days' work at Cincinnati studios shooting a tourists' VR experience.

The exhibition is almost empty, which I guess is normal for a Thursday morning this time of year. There was an older couple wandering around behind me at the Forum but since we've come inside they've racked up a fair bit of distance; they're back in Spaghetti Westerns by my reckoning. The school group is still outside; I'd be able to hear their limbs smacking against each other, the sound of coat on coat and bags of crisps rustling in their pockets if they were close.

With no one around to make me self-conscious, I glance at the shark and then at where the camera must be hidden in the wall.

My face stretches into the terror I've been asked for. My breath creaks out from my throat as I mime a scream. I sweep imagined water from in front of me, fleeing my predator. This happens in my body and on the screen at exactly the same time. I escape the shark and the screen changes. In space, I float in zero gravity. I look at the sweeping indigo all around me, salted as it is, with the stars.

On the metro back into the city, I peel a tangerine in my lap. It's my sixth tangerine in 49 hours, which is as long as we've been in Rome. Each segment resists my teeth just long enough before bursting. The juice is a cold shock, as if the tangerine absorbed November's chill whilst suspended in my handbag, and is releasing it now into my mouth.

Bethany is waiting for me across the road as I emerge from underground. She holds two ice creams, dripping jauntily onto each of her hands. It is objectively not the weather for ice cream but I can almost hear her say, *when in Rome...*

She spreads her arms out for a hug, oblivious to – or not bothered by – the precarity of the double scoops. I lean down to her in her chair and she kisses me. Her mouth is wet and cold like the tangerine. I keep my eyes on her grin as I straighten back up, swiftly. We've never been to Italy before so I don't know where we sit on the spectrum of normal-and-thus-invisible to so-different-it's-dangerous. The guidebook says ambiguous things about Rome being *conservative*. I don't want the afternoon to be ruined by the wrong kind of look from someone passing by but if I don't look, I won't see them.

'I got you chocolate one side and lemon the other,' she says. 'The guidebook said gelato and sorbet was a *typically* Italian mix, so...'

'Is it wrong that I'm having a great time?' I ask.

'No babe,' she says. 'It's not.'

We have a predetermined schedule for the trip, with the days divided into time together and time apart, in which Bethany can rest and I do the things that shitty public transport or cobbles or not-enough-interest-in-relation-to-the-energetic-cost means she can't or won't do with me. My time alone reads like a checklist of niche interest and touristy bits: *Colosseum, Cincinnati, Borghesi/Bird House (garden with Beth?), Protestant Cemetery (cats!), Trevi Fountain, Montemartini, Forum Romanum.* Our time together goes like this: *pizza, wine, let's-see-time, cheese, Settimo Cielo?, pasta.* Then in a section kind of on its own: *Lainey's Mum.*

The last time we "did a city break" was in Paris four years ago with Annette and Jem. Jem is one of those people who barrels through everything with maximum enthusiasm and intensity, including breaks away. Her good health is almost domineering.

In Paris, she resented that if we wanted to nip up the Notre Dame, we needed to crack on while Beth was napping at the hotel, how time allotted to stair climbing couldn't be whenever she fancied. It frayed her a little, that when Bethany was with us we would pootle, or sit still in a *jardin* and watch the world go by. She didn't like that during time-Beth-rests – if she really did want to bomb round the Louvre and up the Eiffel tower in that one long weekend – she couldn't. We had to work with time Beth had scheduled, but wasn't there for.

'How do you deal with this every day?' Jem asked, as we waited for Beth to join us one afternoon. We were at a table outside a cafe, and Jem had a macaron in her hand, the sun glinting on the cobbles like sugar glaze on a bun. 'All this planning when you're supposed to be off work... the rigidity of it, it's exhausting.'

'Well Beth did the logistics,' I pointed out. She'd collated our emailed wishlists and sat with a map of the city three weekends in a row. 'I guess sticking to it means she has a good time too. What's the problem?'

I didn't say it in an aggy way, but Annette's lips pursed up and her tone was extra bright when she spoke.

'Oof, let's not have conflict on holiday.' She stress-swallowed and smiled. 'Jemmy, I can't finish this bear's claw. Will you help me out?'

'It's not like it's any more flexible for Bethany,' I said, unable to let it go. 'She has to rest when she has to rest.'

'Really Jem,' Annette said. Her voice was only marginally louder, and she was tearing her pastry into chunks, proffering them at both of us in an insistent but under-stated way. 'It's delicious! I'm just full. What about you Lainey; fancy a bite?'

3.

Jem and I went out the week before Rome to this place off Soho square round the corner from where she works. The restaurant was decorated for Halloween and my elbows kept meeting the elbows of the person at the table next to me. I tried to work out the most cost-effective way of getting full off of small plates and also a bit drunk, but Jem ordered for us both and told me she was paying.

'How you feeling about your trip?' she asked, when our food came. 'Have you worked out how to take your mum yet?'

'We're using make-up pots,' I replied. 'I've bought a bunch of glitters and other powdery things we can mix her into.'

'Oh fuck,' she said, her eyebrows shooting up. She smudged some tomato gel from her spoon into the piece of tiny bread in her hand and spoke through the mouthful. 'Will that go in the hold, or in your hand luggage?'

'We're only taking carry-on.'

She looked up in time to see my face, and reached out across the table right away, gripping my hand with hers, slightly greasy from the food but we didn't care. She held me with her eyes, in the way she does that reminds me of why I love her so much, regardless.

4.

Bethany's always got chatting to whoever we sit by on trains or planes. When we land, she'll be swapping social media profiles with her neighbour, armed with a dinner invite if they're local and always with a story to tell me in the taxi to our hotel. On the flight to Rome I got three songs into my playlist and feel asleep. She was sat next to a pilgrim who was also an accountant and I could hear her, asking questions as I drifted.

'I'm quite intrigued, actually,' Beth said to me, while we waited for everyone else to get off the plane before us. 'I know we've decided against Vatican City, but apparently there's a church not far from there that has Mary Magdalene's foot inside. It's one of the holiest places in Italy because she was the first to walk where Jesus had stood, after he rose again. So her foot kind of sucked up his foot and got all sacred.'

'You don't even believe in all that!'

'Well I do and I don't... But what do you reckon? We have a slot scheduled tomorrow morning to do something spontaneous if I have energy. Can we go rub it?'

'The foot?'

'Yeh.'

I looked at her, amused. 'Of course, if that's what you want.'

'It is,' she said, and she looked out the window at the runway, eyes gleaming.

5.

Mum went really slowly and by the end – honestly – I felt relieved for her, when she was dead. I was relieved for me too, which was a secret that hurt so much. It complicated the grief I dropped into, where the ground had been cleaved open, where my mum had gone. Except we didn't bury her; she was cremated. She went in a pot that's sat in the corner of my bedroom for ten years and now – in two weeks time – I will turn 40, the age she was when she got sick. This feels like a right old double whammy of things to be dealing with, and Beth tells me I have started to compulsively eat citrus fruit and talk in my sleep.

When we were in Paris, Annette WhatsApped her mother a picture of every meal we ate. We met Annette's mother at her thirtieth, and it was immediately clear where her unsettled relationship to both hunger and interpersonal tension had come from, beyond just being white and a woman. Annette's mum had sat with Beth for half an hour asking questions about her family and her training though, and didn't mention her chair once. She sent us both birthday cards every year since, and a kitschy butter dish when we managed to buy our house. Annette is like her in that way, too. She remembers things; she makes you feel like things count.

Jem didn't get involved in the food photos, but she called her mum from one of the makeshift book stands on the bank of the Seine, to ask if she wanted a particular copy of a Simone de Beauvoir the rest of us had never heard of. Jem's mother's known me since I was five, and doesn't send birthday cards in the post, but does send me links to petitions I always start to sign until they ask me to make an account, and I just can't face the extra emails I'll inevitably end up receiving.

All this is to say the thing I miss most about having a mum is calling her up to communicate stuff that doesn't matter.

Like how in Italy, you eat a creamy scoop of gelato with a crisp fruit sorbet together; how every woman you see in a painting or carved from rock, has layers of drapery spilling from her waist; it looks so heavy to carry clothes like that around; that there's white stone everywhere you turn; and that yes, Mum was right when she told her sister Rome was beautiful, and this big, sweaty city – ancient buildings round every corner, traffic like you wouldn't be-lieve, throngs of people taking selfies, worn out trainers and backpacks and commuters and kids – was where – in an ideal world – she'd like to be *sprinkled*.

I feel like I am on my way to getting old and I'm an-gry my mum didn't and I also really feel like I should've dealt with that by now. Beth is Beth, and she rolls her eyes when I say shit like this, or she kisses me, or makes me a tea, or sends me links to therapists. We've both had therapy, and I know grief isn't a hole in the ground that closes over once you've climbed back out. Mum's been a number in my phone I've not called for a decade. Before that, a decade of phonecalls about chemo and surgery and groceries and random shit I had for lunch. Now it's my job to sprinkle her.

6.

Beth was too tired for spontaneity the day after we arrived, so we didn't go rub Mary Magdalene's foot. She slept and I scrolled the news on socials. I ask her if she wants to go now, instead of committing to the slot in our timetable scheduled for pizza, and she looks at me like, *obviously pizza*.

According to the schedule's colour-coded squares – laminated using the copy room at the school she works in, and placed at all times in my back pocket – we will now drift to a piazza round the corner – not so far we cannot deal with the cobbles – and sit outside a restaurant that has heaters (in case the interior is too narrow to get her chair into, because even though she can walk, and it can be folded, the proprietor will panic and Beth will feel like she's glowing and expanding and everyone is staring, and I will overcompensate and we won't enjoy the cheese puddling across salty dough that we have gone there for) to eat pizza and for me to drink copious lunchtime wine.

In my ear at the table she whispers that if we had gone to see Mary Magdalene she wouldn't have the energy to do what she wants to do after the food. I ask her what that is and she whispers it's to go down on me with the curtains of our hotel window open, and I tell her let's, and the wine and the warmth from the heater make me kind of forget that I don't know if kissing her in public is a good idea, and my tongue is in her mouth and she tastes of tomatoes and gorgonzola.

On our bed later, I think of the green screen: of the

shark and the open dark of space. I want so much to disappear my thoughts into Beth's mouth, her lips doing that thing like sucking and kissing both at once between my legs. I don't want to ruin the moment. I try to relax, to visualise the deep purple all around me, the stars and stars and stars. She can tell though, and she wriggles up the bed alongside me. She kisses my mouth and now she tastes like me, a different salty, and she says, 'You feeling weird, babe?'

'It's all the containers,' I say, only knowing what the words will be as they come out. 'She's been in that bloody urn all this time and now she's in nine different jars and pots and... I don't want to tip her out.'

She nests her head in my armpit and wraps an arm and a leg across me.

'You don't have to, Lainey. We can always take her home again.'

7.

At Settimo Cielo, I decide to just do it. In my handbag, the containers have been rattling ever since we arrived. Beth's wheels won't work on sand – those ones were too expensive for us – and we don't want to leave her chair unattended. So she sits at the top of the beach and waits.

The sky above the sea is how a sky would be on a green screen: blue as blue with one or two perfect clouds trundling serenely across it. I wait for an actor to tell me what to mime but there are no instructions forthcoming.

The ashes I have mixed in with glitter eyeshadows sparkle as I chuck them into the sea. Of course, they don't just fly effortlessly away and I am dusted with flecks of blue and green and gold, and bits of my mum's burnt body. The sand next to me is too. This makes me laugh and cry at once, and I feel like a child and I think about the relief I felt that my mum had died because that way of dying had been so horrible. God I miss her. There is no one about;

it is, after all, November. If this was VR, the scene would change; I would have escaped.

I've mixed a bit of Mum into a cream foundation and I'm pretty annoyed with myself trying to work out what to do with that. I end up scooping it out and getting my shoes and the ankles of my trousers all wet trying to wash the last bits off my hand and away.

We get a shot of grappa at the beach bar afterwards to toast her. I drink three of them, and although I couldn't tell you how I am feeling, I can feel that Beth is exhausted. I order us a horribly expensive taxi straight back to the hotel so we can avoid the bus. Maybe I talk that night in my sleep; I don't know.

8.

Beth told Jem and Annette about the accountant pilgrim in the group chat when we first landed and they've obviously only just looked at the messages properly because while we're sat at our final breakfast a stream of texts come in from them.

Mary Magdalene was a lesbian too! Jem types.

Queer Biblical babes for the win! Annette adds. And then; *Although that is just a theory Jemmy!!*

There are some laughing face emojis. An article from some academic journal about Mary LGBTQ Magdalene. Annette sends us a picture of their brunch.

Having a cheeky croissant – so indulgent!

Hope you're doing ok out there.

Tell us about what you did with your mum if you want to.

We love you

I tell Beth I feel bad that the one thing she wanted to do – rub the foot in the church – is the thing we haven't done.

'We've done loads of things I wanted. And we can come back.'

I unpeel another tangerine, its waxy skin curling onto

my plate. I feed Beth a segment and she sucks on my fingers a little as they toy with the edge of her mouth. I close my eyes for a moment. At the edge of the city, the sea floats my mother away.

Blood, Body, Wings

Vicky K Pointing

You first saw her when you were seven, on a family trip abroad. It was a disaster; too warm for mother, who wilted irritably under the sun. As if the heat wasn't enough, one day you'd turned into the path of an oncoming lamppost, slamming your head against it. From your confusing new position on the pavement, you took in a broad stretch of blue sky punctured by your mother's furious face. She hissed at you to get up, that you were a stupid, clumsy girl. You tried, but your body wouldn't do as it was told, and the world kept flickering to black streaked with red, splashes of colour that flitted, insect-like, across your vision.

Once the flashes stopped, your gaze was drawn to the shadows behind your mother, a sleek sweep of darkness cutting down from the edge of a building. Something blacker than the shade moved within it, folding inwards and then out like the beating of a wing. It pulsed and bloomed into a woman, her edges smudged, face turned into the dark. She reached a hand towards you, slender fingers pale as the moon. Your father stepped in front of her, the light returning with him. He swung you up to standing and held you there until your knees remembered how to work.

"No harm done," he said, wiping a little blood from the scratch on your face.

You glanced into the shadows as he led you away. They were empty, and your heart felt just as hollow.

That evening after dinner, your mother wanted a bath, but the water ran with a rusty tinge.

"Old pipes," your father said, dismissing her complaints with a wave of his hand.

Your mother scowled, pouting and sighing until you

arrived back home, when she announced she'd never go abroad again.

There were no holidays at all for a while. Your mother kept getting headaches and had to lie in your parents' bedroom, in the dark, for days at a time. You didn't mind. Your father took you to school, brought you home, and at mealtimes he summoned you to eat toast or soup or spaghetti hoops, served with a frown. He let you play and watch whatever you liked on TV and stay up later than you should. Eventually your mother's headaches stopped, and when he told you she was better, you put on a big smile, knowing it was expected.

You spent the next summer, and several more after that, in cottages near the coast with your parents, pretending to enjoy long afternoons of board games while rain murmured a steady incantation that blurred the windows, stealing the world outside. Eventually, even your mother grew tired of that, and finally consented to another holiday overseas. You'd stay in a house on a farm, a short drive to culture and cafes and bright little shops, with warm evenings, good food, red wine for mother.

You spent the weeks leading up to the plane ride holding your breath, doing your best to be invisible. In the darkness of an early July morning, you piled into the car with your suitcase, plugged in your headphones and pretended to sleep; a well-practised strategy to avoid becoming the focus of your parents' low bickering. You spent the flight with your gaze glued to the horizon, searching for the first thin slice of another country peering out above the sea.

The dirt road to the house was rough, and the car stirred up the dust of three weeks with no rain, flinging some of it through your open window. You felt the excitement of a new place and stared out at a sprawling field of sunflowers, thick stemmed, their rough faces turned to the light. You don't remember what your room was like, only the silence and darkness that night. You wanted to sleep with a lamp on, so kept reading after your parents went to bed, but your mother crossed your room like an uninvited spirit and switched the light off. You watched the faint glow of her white nightdress recede to nothing.

The next day, you spent a little time in the fields, tipping your head back to bathe your face in the heat of the sun. Your mother would have liked to rest in the shade, but your father had a schedule. Every morning he swept you both into the car and drove into town or to the sorts of places he thought you should go: a ruined castle, a museum, a hissing wind-whipped beach. Once, he took you to a pottery and, while your mother cooed over a dull, expensive vase, you found yourself wandering past shelves filled with palm-sized, long-limbed creatures, wings draped over skeletal bodies, eyes huge, dark and uncaring. Fairies perhaps, but not the reassuring kind. Some had sharp little teeth. All had claws. You bought one, clutching it all the way back to the farm.

That night you woke with an ache in your belly and found blood on your pyjamas when you stumbled to the toilet. You sat, exuberant and sore, pressing your feet into the cold floor tiles, until your mother pushed the door open and stood at the threshold, arms crossed.

You explained. You did your best to keep the pride out of your voice, knowing she'd only sneer, but really you were pleased. Maybe because your body was doing what it should, and a change in you had been marked in blood, colossal, indisputable, a truth beyond her reach.

Without a word, your mother stepped to the bathroom cabinet and took out a handful of nappy-like pads, dropping them at your feet.

"I don't need any extra washing," she said, turning her back and pulling the door closed behind her.

"She's fine," you heard her say in response to your father's worried voice.

You knew that other people's mothers were kind. Other people's mothers stayed when they needed them, smiled and spoke softly. You could almost hear that, almost feel someone stroking your hair, moving it away from your face with moon-pale fingers.

You tidied up, washed your hands, went to bed. You placed your fairy by the bedside lamp and switched it off, the light leaving an imprint on your eyelids. The air was hot, and you thought someone whispered your name, but it was only an insect buzzing softly past your ear.

*

Years pass. Your father leaves, and you sit your mother down to explain that you are all she has. Since then, the two of you have progressed, if not to peace then at least a truce, an agreement to each pack away your cruellest weapons.

Now, you're at university, two years in, living with a happy crowd from your course and too busy relishing new knowledge and new friendships to go home more than once or twice a year. But you and your mother have decided to meet up for a night away, in a small town, somewhere pretty.

You arrive at a B and B, take photos of each other grinning by a window, pointing at the view, but you're distracted. You excuse yourself to the bathroom, sit on the edge of the toilet, press a hand against your stomach. You're late. You're never late. Ever since that lonely, triumphant night in a foreign bathroom, you've been able to predict the first-day cramps almost to the hour. But they've forsaken you. Instead, dread snakes and coils behind your palm, dense and black.

"Come on, I'm starving," your mother calls, and you open the bathroom door, doing your best to look light-hearted. You pull on a summer jacket, head into the street.

You met him in a club. When he spotted you, he was chatting up your friend, and walked away from her so abruptly that her mouth dropped open, gaping comically as he introduced himself to you. He was fun, cocky, attentive. You were flattered. But six months on his affection is two-dimensional, a shallow puddle of desire when you could drown him ten times over. You could love him, but you won't, no matter what happens next.

As you walk beside your mother, you stare at your hands, suddenly alien, your arms swinging, legs moving boldly of their own accord. Your body has hijacked you for its own rebellious intention, dragging you along, as you struggle to escape its current. Everything feels distant, separated from you by a great depth of water. Air escapes your mouth as it forms a soundless protest.

You know what it is to be unwanted, and you don't want this. You were certain that every cell of you felt the same, shuddered at the thought of playing host, the possibility of foetal limbs gliding blindly in the dark, a second heartbeat in frantic echo of your own.

"You're so fussy about your food," your mother says, startling you. She wrinkles her nose at another menu in another restaurant window, signalling her rejection by walking away. You don't bother replying, only grit your teeth.

After you've eaten, you're swept through lively streets. You step aside to catch your breath and spot a funfair, a welcome mass of light and noise. Your mother waits impatiently while you hook a duck, then grumpily accepts the oversized teddy bear you win, although she insists you carry it. You do until you spot the rollercoaster and find yourself drawn to its sweeping curves.

"Just one go," you say, wanting to feel something other than fear, or at least, to feel it for another reason.

"I'm not standing on my own all night," your mother says.

"I won't be long."

"What about the bear?"

The operator straps the teddy in next to you, grinning. The bar comes down and you cling to it tightly. As you creak up the first stretch of track towards a long drop your eyes water, the wind snatching at your face, tugging your hair. At the top, you open your mouth wide to scream. Air floods your throat, and you think of the night you woke up choking in your university flat. You reached for the fairy that still sat by your bedside, but your fingers couldn't close on its familiar, jagged shape. In the morning, there were hollow fragments of porcelain strewn across the carpet, revealing hidden, disintegrating parts of something real: an abdomen, a wing.

"I didn't think you liked rollercoasters," your mother says, when you're back on the ground.

You shrug.

Back at the B and B, you tuck the bear into your mother's bed while she washes her face, as a carefree daughter would.

"Very funny," she says, when she steps out of the bathroom.

You find it hard to fall asleep, and then you dream of the darkest shadows. A woman emerges, at first only half-formed, impossible to look at directly. Her image shifts and settles when she touches your face, her fingertips chilled and clammy. You open your mouth, and something flutters out damply from your throat, swooping after the woman as she turns away. You hear your name, and the darkness is banished. You blink at your mother's anxious face outlined by the sudden light of the bedside lamp.

"You were gasping in your sleep," she says.

You sit up, turn your head, but there's no-one in the room except the two of you, only red streaks that quickly fade to black. You press a fist to your stomach, which has just started to ache.

Bothy

Miranda Roszkowski

The first cold drop of rain fell as she started the climb. The clouds above, gnarled and purple-black with menace, blocked out most of the fading light so Jen had to squint to make out the mound on the *brae*. It was always uphill, the bothy. It had been the same at Staoineag and the Glen. They made you work for it.

The wind snapped her hair into her eyes. Shaking off the thought of her warm flat in York, she scrunched her fists inside the lambswool gloves that once belonged to her Highlander grandmother and pushed on into the wind. The gravel underfoot slipped away as she placed her sodden walking boots one in front of the other.

This would be her third night in a bothy, pronounced, she'd learned, both-ee like *bother*. The free shelters were described on the website as "like camping without a tent" but had a roof, sometimes a fire and were known as places you could meet other walkers. Not that she'd come to make friends, but it had surprised Jen how much she'd ached for other humans after a day of cracking her bones against the wind with no other soul in sight, her thoughts swirling as fast as the near-gales up here. On her first night, she'd arrived around five in the afternoon to find Isobel and Eamon stoking a fire, ready to tell tales from their lives in Inverness and how they liked to "get lost for the weekend now and then". They'd been joined later by Stan, a bricklayer from Southampton who, like Jen, had never experienced bothies before, but had come to get his head straight after "a mad break up" and an "even madder summer, man."

She'd left most of the conversation to them, nodding when she needed to, laughing at the jokes. She had no stories of her own to tell; after eight years, everything – her friends, opinions, the holiday let in Filey – had been shared. And now, here she was, alone the night before her 35th birthday, nothing but a half empty flat waiting for her and no idea what was next. She did not mention the birthday.

When they'd asked what brought her to the Highlands, she'd just mumbled something about summers with her grandmother. It made her dizzy to think that six months ago, she'd known exactly where her path in life would take her, take *them*. How five months ago, Jamie had rolled over in the morning and with a few short words knocked her totally off course. When she muttered generalisations about the scenery to her fellow walkers, she did not articulate how four months ago the legs that today carried her over bogs and crags and jumped rivers, would barely hold her upright. And how one month ago, with the pain not fading but now much more like shame, and the Big Birthday looming, she'd cancelled all plans and told the few friends she'd retained in the split she was going abroad. Each damp day in the Highlands she wondered whether Ibiza might have been a more fulfilling choice.

At that first bothy, she'd waved goodbye cheerfully enough in the morning, thanks for breakfast, good luck and that. Each step afterwards she felt the cold absence of company seeping further into her bones. Many Happy Returns. Her birthday night was spent just her, a draughty cabin and a breathtaking view over a valley with no-one to share it. She found firewood but couldn't get it lit. Strange animal screeches came intermittently from the wood behind. Closer, further away. And close again.

After shivering all night, her walk the next day was slower, her stumbles on uneven ground more frequent. The wind was ice-sharp, pricking at her cheeks. When her boot got stuck in a bog that was definitely not on the map, it took her over half an hour to wriggle out from the mud, all the while praying she wouldn't have to unlace her boot to escape then squelch across the deserted moors in socks. Three miles of red-faced stomping later, it struck her how lucky it was she'd been able to rescue herself, because what would happen otherwise? If she'd got sucked in as far as her waist? She'd pulled her coat tighter and got her head down. The weather worsened. At no point had she felt a revelation coming on. Profound moments were not on the menu today.

At last, she reached the door of the tiny cottage. A deep growl of thunder told her it was just in time. She needed two goes for her numb fingers to work the door handle and it was only as she stepped into the blackness that she realised how small the space was, room for one or two at most. No sound – empty, and, she checked her watch, at 9pm, light fading, it wasn't likely anyone else would turn up. She gave her eyes a second to adjust, but this bothy was entirely dark. Not a shard of light penetrated the thick stone walls or slates above.

It felt warmer as she closed the door to the moaning wind. She fumbled for her pocket torch. The beam was strong but narrow and she had to move slowly to make out a sleep-shelf on the left. She unfurled her bed roll and peeled her sleeping bag from the cocoon pack attached to her small rucksack. Just as well she'd had the sense to fill up her flask from the steam a few miles back, no sign of water here. It was the most basic bothy yet, but she was glad to be safe – a louder, angrier, roar of thunder signalled the storm was setting in. She didn't remember reading anything about that in the weather report.

Her grandmother would have known the signs, Jen thought. She used to say something about the light, about sensing the direction of the wind by watching the grass. What had Jen cared at the time? Why had she imagined that now, thirty-odd years later, she would have the same instincts as her favourite but long-dead grandparent, de-spite having spent the last decade city-bound? And how did she fool herself into thinking that walking until her feet bled would somehow take away from that tarry ache that she felt in her chest every waking minute? Her grandmother would have had something to say about that, too, Jen was sure. But her memories gave her no answers, and there was only the whine of the storm to keep her company tonight.

Too tired to unpack the tiny portable cooker, Jen settled for cheese and a few crackers followed by a Mars bar as her dinner, and decided to get straight into bed. She would have another go tomorrow, her last day, to find the resolution that she had been hoping for, escape those thoughts that had pursued her over waterfalls and through craggy outcrops. Being alone was not such a good therapy, she had a sneaking thought, when you are trying not to worry about Being Alone. Five months and still had no idea why Jamie had left. Had there been someone else? They had been "too comfortable" he'd said. How can a person be too comfortable? She still felt the punch when she thought about it. She sighed loudly and hoisted herself onto the bed.

Then she froze. A sound had come from the corner, a sort of groan. There was someone there. She held her breath for a moment. The sound of weight shifting, turning. Silence. She continued to breathe lightly. After a while, she shone her torch across the room. There, only about two meters distance from her, was a heap, a person, large and lying in a dark blanket facing the opposite wall. A man, most likely.

Jen was suddenly conscious of how far away she was from help. Not having phone signal was excellent for avoiding social media accounts of ex-boyfriends who seemed to be having no problem moving on. But what *would* happen if she got in trouble? Her bothy planning counted on knowing who she was sharing with, and worst come to worst, knowing she could wild camp outside. But the storm was crackling now, the wind thumping the door. Would the man be friendly? What if he was drunk? She wasn't the only one that came to the Highlands to forget their troubles. What if he was drunk, and strong, and lonely in that dangerous way?

Jen took a mental inventory of the contents of her bag. She didn't even have aerosol deodorant to spray in an assailant's eyes. She took a breath, understanding she might be irrational. But. Safest thing was not to wake him.

She lowered herself down on top of her sleeping bag. And out of nowhere, she sneezed.

A rustle. "Is someone there?" The man's voice was soft, quite high-pitched, maybe old. Southern.

"Yeah?" Her attempt to sound confident was unsuccessful.

"Oh," the voice sounded surprised. Possibly even wary. "You bin here long?"

He made the "here" sound like "ear".

"I..." she cleared her throat. "Just got in as it turned nine."

A weak glow came from around his head-height. "Twenty-three past now," he said. "And there's me asleep for at least an hour."

The man didn't sound too threatening. "Sorry I woke you," she said.

"No bother, I just reckoned I'd be on my tod, such a tiny place, you know."

She couldn't quite place the accent, somewhere West Country, maybe.

"Good day?" The voice came again. He seemed to have woken up fully, rolling over to face her by the sound of it.

She was surprised to hear her voice crack when she spoke. "It was a bit tough, to be honest."

Silence for a moment. Then he spoke. "Can take you unawares can't it?" He said. "Round here."

She didn't reply, found herself biting her lip.

"I come every year," he continued. "Walk the trail like we used to. Me and Sheila."

Jen sniffed.

"I show her pictures when I get back but she don't really remember. Bit too far gone now."

Jen rolled onto her side. In the dark, they faced each other. "I'm sorry."

"What can any of us do? If that's the way He decides it's gonna go. Upstairs, you know?"

They were both quiet for a while. Jen cleared her throat. "It would be nice to think *someone* had a plan. Sometimes."

A chuckle. "You going far then?"

"Fort Worth."

"Past Lough Leven?"

"Yeah, and Landavra."

"Best views in the country. You can't look at them without knowing that the Big Man has a plan."

Jen said nothing for a time. "I'm not sure about the Big Man," she said in the end.

The wind was quieter now, still bumping faintly against the door, rain tapping the roof. Its rhythm lulled her deeper into her sleeping sack.

The man yawned. "Well, don't miss the view. Life-changing."

"That's what I need."

"That so?" The man was quiet this time. Jen could feel the weight of her eyelids. Just as she closed them, the man replied.

"Whatever you have to do. My advice? Don't waste any time. Life has a habit of sneakin' away from you."

Jen would not normally let unsolicited advice go unchallenged. But she said nothing, and let herself melt into the warm, strange comfort of the darkness. The humming wind soothed her to sleep.

The next day she woke to stillness. No wind, nor rain on the roof. She cracked her shoulders and rolled her head. Then she stood, soundlessly packed her bag in the gloom and left the bothy, closing the door quietly so as not to wake the man snoring in the corner. Outside, the grass was damp with dew, droplets sparkling in the morning light. The air was fresh on her tongue as she took a long breath in.

Then she was away.

Water Back

Rob Schofield

Some want to chat, while others wish you would pour their drink and shut the fuck up. Both are fine with me. Some like to keep a conversation going for hours, dipping in and out whenever they need a refill. The astute ones know to recap when they pick up where they left off. There are yet others who are prepared to pass the time of day and exchange pleasantries while they wait, but they're not interested. That's okay: it's a bar and they are customers. I appreciate it if they smile, make the right noises, but it's not a deal breaker. With some of them it's like hero worship. You'd think I was stripping down to my undies on a stormy night at Blackpool, ready to save a drowning man. Or woman, although it does skew towards the male of the species.

I was working behind the bar when he appeared. As much as you keep an eye out for who's in and who's not, who's sitting where they shouldn't and who's visiting the establishment for the first time, you can't be on hand for the arrival of every poor sod that flops onto a stool in search of salvation. Also, that day, it wasn't a good one for me. I hadn't slept, the car was being temperamental, my washing machine was on the blink, and there was the matter of Mum having died a month ago and Dad six before that. The first three things I might share with some of the usual crowd, but what with the dead parents and grief and unresolved emotions, I wasn't in the frame of mind where I might bare my soul to a person who exists in that zone where friendship, acquaintance, and business lock horns. I was walking a tightrope of tears, and I don't mean the kind you can dab at with the corner of a tissue. Huge, gasping sobs were building up in my chest, and try as I might to maintain a professional façade, I was this much away from banshee mode. Those clever types I mentioned earlier were giving me as wide a berth as thirst would allow.

'Pint of Peroni, shot of Stoli, water back,' says a voice I haven't heard before. There was a warmth to it, like he was drying his feet by a fire and revisiting a pleasant memory.

'Ey?' I look up from the mixers. One day some fucker will order bitter lemon.

'Peroni, sorry. Forgot where I was for a moment.'

'Where did you think you were?' My money was on somewhere in the U S of A.

'Across the pond,' he says, quick as a flash. 'The Big Apple. Nu Yoik.' That's how he said it: like a person trying to do the accent.

'A transatlantic traveller? You're a rare breed around here.' I dug about for a Peroni glass. We've got a few, but most of them get nicked so we're careful about giving them out.

'I like that.' He points at the glass.

'They go home in handbags. Here you go.' I placed the beer in front of him.

He nodded and licked his lips.

'Knock yourself out,' I said. 'No one's watching.'

'You never know,' he says, all serious. 'I don't like to drink on the clock.'

'You're not from the council?' We'd had one or two issues with our risk assessments.

'Nothing like that. Just sizing up a job.'

'In a bar?'

'As good a place as any,' he said, continuing his surveillance of the lager.

'Somewhere to think.'

'Spot on,' he says. 'A place where one can assess the state of the world.'

'Another barroom philosopher,' I said, hand to my chest in mock exasperation; but a moment later, I remembered my woes and felt rotten for being so light-hearted, as though I'd betrayed all I had to worry about.

'And if not the state, then perhaps the weight, which, if you don't mind me saying, you appear to be carrying on your shoulders.'

Our conversation continued for an hour or so, albeit there were gaps while I serviced the regulars and newbies. He left when my back was turned, the pint of Peroni intact on the bar, minus the bubbles. I didn't think about it at the time, but later, when I was sat in the car praying for it to start, I realised that we hadn't spoken about him at all, or not enough for me to give an account of him, were one ever needed. My sketchy recollection is of flawless skin, a blonde crew cut, and a frame which was muscular, but not gym chiselled. As for what kind of person he was, I have no clue other than it felt good to be in his company. More than good: relaxing, comforting, positive. And that's rare, don't you think? I felt like that when I met Deano – like he got me and appreciated me – but no one before or after that. I lost touch with Deano.

I phoned in sick the next day. Midway through what would have been my afternoon shift, I found myself wishing I'd gone in. I wasn't feeling guilty – a zero-hours contract confers instant and ongoing absolution – but I was bored and fed up with the car/laundry/Mum and Dad situation. A therapist once told me it's important to rec-ognise when you need help, and if you can do that, you've taken the first step. Everything's a fucking journey with those people, but some of us our cars are knackered and it's not so easy to get from A to B, never mind the far reaches of the alphabet. Okay, that's a long-winded way of me telling you that I was thinking about the stranger and whether he had reappeared at the bar. We'd hit it off – not like that – and what with connections being difficult to make, I don't mind admitting I was hoping I might have found a friend. Isn't there a rule about that in the trade? Barkeeping 101? Maybe, but life is more important than work; and if you're not in agreement I respectfully suggest you take your voyeurism elsewhere.

I spent another night lying awake for fear of sleeping in. As it was, Matthew phoned nice and early to check if I was fit. Paula, who does the opposite shift to me and doesn't mind pulling a double when I'm unavailable, had contracted a virus, which we all know means couldn't be arsed going in. I could hear in Matthew's voice that he was shitting himself at the prospect of having to lift a finger, but fear not! I was happy, nay keen, to ride in on my charger and save the day, having reason other than lining his pockets to grace the bar with my presence.

There was a kid in black trackies and grey hoodie, all arms and legs, at the bus stop. His kecks were hanging off him, ripped and covered in God knows what. He had a filthy backpack slung over his shoulder, and when he grinned there were gaps where you and I have teeth. He made the driver wait while I ran across the road, raising a fist in solidarity as he trudged up the steps to the top deck. You put yourself at the mercy of these apps, which never tell you when something's running early, when you should try having faith in people around you, even the scruffy ones that some of us – including you, be honest – dismiss as druggies rather than consider they might be as scared and vulnerable as you. Don't we all want to go through life unbothered, with a teensy bit of hope and a shot at happiness? He looked like he didn't have a bean beyond his bus fare, but he'd done that for me.

I watched Matthew through a window when I arrived. He was dealing beer mats onto the tables like the world's least motivated croupier. The spring returned to his step when I pushed through the door. I started to tell him about the kid, but he was out the other way within two minutes, saying something about the wholesalers. I don't know why he was going there. I'd stocked up two days earlier and ours isn't a clientele reliant on sundries. Beer and hard liquor, yes; peanuts and crisps, maybe. Food? What's wrong with peanuts and crisps? You get the picture.

Time dragged along with the clock at the end of the optics. You can torture yourself with a lot of thoughts from one second to the next. I wiped down the bar top and did it again. I moved on to the tables where dirty streaks told me that Matthew hadn't been up to the job. My eyes were weeping with cheap detergent from his beloved wholesaler. My nostrils were raw with it. I made myself a coffee and stared at the main doors until the brew made a beeline for my bladder. He was sitting at the bar – same stool – when I came back from the loo.

'Pint of Peroni, shot of Stoli, water back.' I cocked my thumb and finger like a pistol and pointed it at him. 'Sorry, don't know where that came from.' I holstered the gun with a shrug.

'One out of three. Surprise me.' He played along, doing the accent again.

'You remembered?' I reached for a Peroni glass.

'And so did you.'

'Part of the job,' I said.

'I know what you mean,' he replied.

He let me tell him about my bus stop saviour, nodding and frowning as I gabbled on.

'Something went wrong.' He was peering at the glass again, hands nowhere near it.

'How do you mean?'

'Who's looking out for him?'

'Who's looking out for anyone?'

'Something's broken. Tell me where you saw him.'

'Why?'

'Maybe I can help.'

'You going to give him money? Find him a place to live?'

'I can try. I can listen. You could have listened.'

'I've got enough on my plate.' I polished a clean glass and looked for another to work on.

'Like what?'

'My car broke down. The washing machine is fucked. I

told you about Mum and Dad.'

'Machines can be fixed. The other stuff you can get help with.'

'Assuming you've the time and money.' I pointed at his glass. 'What's wrong with it?'

'Nothing. Sorry,' he said, 'I know you have your troubles.'

'No sweat.' But he'd irked me. I should have followed the kid upstairs and said a proper thank you.

Someone, by which I mean me, had to cover Paula's shift. Enough regulars crawled in to keep me busy, with Matthew back from his travels and coiled like a spring in the office for backup. He can pour a drink when the toilet needs unblocking, but otherwise he's fucking useless, and I'd rather fly solo. I hadn't noticed my new barroom buddy slipping away, but it didn't bother me: he hadn't lived up to our first meeting and even though it might not have been fair, I blamed him for that. I can't say that I was happy to see him as I pulled down the shutters on another day, but I was intrigued enough not to mind when he fell in step with me. The air was damp, heavy, Dickensian. It might as well have been raining, or snowing, since it was cold enough. Amidst the sirens, there was the suggestion of wind. I could have been enjoying a nightcap while putting the world to rights, but Matthew's not the type. Homeward bound is what I was, and if this feller wanted to tag along, that was fine with me.

He hadn't said where he had come from, and I hadn't asked. Nothing about him screamed local, but he knew his way around and didn't complain about me taking the long way home. We walked slow, unsteady. I was wired and exhausted and in no rush to get back to the flat. I wandered around the edge of the bus station, then went inside.

'Looking for someone?' he asked.

'The kid from this morning.'

'Why would we find him here?'

'He was on the bus.'

'That was then. He could be anywhere.'

'You're right. I don't know what I'm doing half the time. I'm knackered and I need my bed.'

He paused by my jalopy, flattened a palm on the bonnet and pursed his lips. I turned around at the top of the steps. He hadn't moved except to close his eyes. You come across all sorts when you work behind a bar, but a man with his hand on a bonnet in the middle of the night was a new one on me. I'd say he was praying if it didn't sound so ridiculous. I stood there waiting until he was done.

'Coffee would be good,' he said, joining me on the steps.

'Sure.' I was trying to come up with a strategy for getting rid of him, but when we sat down with our mugs it was like he'd flicked a switch, and there I was again, pouring out my heart. We talked about death and grief and how time would help. He said I should talk to friends, and didn't mention family, which was just as well seeing as though I'm on my lonesome.

'Did you get on with them?' His mug sat on the table, untouched. I feared he was about to make excuses and skedaddle.

'We were solid, as much as you can be. I had to do a lot for Mum.'

'And now you're feeling lost.'

'There's a void.'

'Bound to be. You've got to think about what's next.'

'But I need time to take it all in.'

'Maybe you do and maybe you don't. Tell me about Deano.'

It had come out of the blue, but now I wonder if this was what it had all been about. We are all wounded – some more than others, like the bus-stop kid – and it's a sad fact that many of us carry multiple injuries. Mum and Dad had taught me well, and it wasn't like I didn't know I'd be an orphan one day; but nobody ever teaches you how to let go of a friendship. A person comes into your life and BANG: you're on the same wavelength. Yes, they laugh at your jokes, and they might like the same books and music, but what's miraculous is when someone knows to let you have your silences without feeling the need to interrupt. They have your back, your front, and your side. There's an inexplicable comfort in their presence and you miss them to the point of physical pain when they're not around. Years later you wonder if they'd take your call, while another part of you won't let go of the belief that they'll be there when push comes to shove. Like, for example, if someone close dies.

'He made an impression on you.'

'Deano?' I blew into my hands, trying to catch a breath. I hadn't realised I'd been talking.

'The way you speak about him, he could be your brother.'

'I wouldn't know.'

'Fair point. A close friend like that, though: what happened?'

'Life.'

'People move on?'

They do when things get intense; when they think it would be a good idea to spend some time apart. They might not want to hurt you, mate – always with the mate, pal, bud – but there comes a time when they would appreciate some space. It'll do you good too, and it won't be forever. I believed him when he said that; and I hold my hand up to thinking too much into things. I see it now, my mistake, but when you're in the middle of it, when you're being cast aside for no reason other than he's bored and wants to shake his life up a bit, you cling on with everything you've got.

'And then Dad died, and Mum died.'

'You said.'

'That's what I mean about life: you can't control the timing.'

'All you can do is keep moving forward.'

'You've said that before.'

'It's worth saying again.'

'But it's not so easy.'

There is so much to deal with when someone dies. Admin, for starters. Certificates, funeral services, interments, cremations. Insurance. Utilities. Bills, bills, bills. And when all that's done, you take stock. There was only me at the crem for Mum. When I'm ready, I'll bury her ashes at Dad's grave. I should sort out a headstone. Who tells you what to write on them?

'It all comes down to grief.' I don't remember him saying anything after that. I should have gone easy on the brandy, but it goes so well with coffee.

The flat was empty when I woke. I peeled my face off the couch and wiped my mouth. Two slices of a pizza I don't remember cooking had found their way under the table. His mug of coffee, topped with scum, rested on the glass. Mine was on the floor next to the pizza. I'm not sure what was worse: the smell, or the taste of last night's booze. I found my watch, said a little prayer that Paula was fit for duty, and crawled to the bathroom. There was a Post-it stuck to the mirror with a list scribbled in pencil:

New battery

Find the kid

Deano?

The question mark was what bugged me while I showered, put in a call about the washer, made porridge, and ate my brekky. I got a neighbour – the one that speaks to me – to push, and we got the car going. That was all it was: the battery. They're not cheap, but they don't break the bank. I drove around town, but I couldn't see the kid. I'll see what he needs when I find him. I don't know what to do about Deano.

Gabriel's Rocket

Lyn Towers

Year 13. At 17 we were expected to know better. He shouldn't have done it, tampering with the experiment in chemistry. "Look Luke. Don't." He just looked at me with those big black eyes, "You're such a wimp Lyn."
  I melted.

Mr Jones, our mad chemistry teacher, had detailed Luke of all people to help set up his demonstration for that afternoon's class; his Halloween experiment, changing water into wine, something to do with change in a chemical's Ph. Luke had been allowed into the locked science storeroom to get the equipment and measure the chemicals Mr Jones was using. Then Luke winked at us all, so we knew he was going to do something. During the experiment he sat open-mouthed as he watched Mr Jones add a pinch of lithium powder to the chemical, then gestured us all to duck when Mr Jones was about to add the second measure. The explosion blew out windows in the lab. I was watching Luke, who had a look of total ecstasy on his face that told me he'd found his passion. Sadly, it wasn't me. No-one was injured except Mr Jones, who was admitted to hospital with burns and cuts to his face and fingers. We were told that he was OK and would be back with us next term.

Luke was expelled. Sent away for corrective treatment. We kept in touch. I knew he wasn't the bad boy people said he was. He was just mischievous. Oh! I was so happy when he started to text me.

When he was released, he didn't come home. Having mixed with lads who knew a bit about explosives his Probation Officer exploited Luke's interest in pyrotechnics and apprenticed him with a gang who set up firework displays at big events. Luke loved it. He texted me all the time about the events he helped set up worldwide; he even went to Vancouver to set up a firework display on a ship in English Bay. He texted me from Sydney where he set up the New Year's show on one of the bridges on the river leading to the harbour.

He changed his name when working with a new gang in Italy. His boss was called Angelo, and one of the pyrotechnicians was Gabriel. Now he'll only respond to Angelo Gabriel, so romantic.

It's now June, 10 years since the accident, he rings. He wants to meet.

"I'm working Gabe," I've started to call him Gabe, "so it'll have to be during my lunch break. I'm at the Council buildings up the road taking the minutes of the Parks Department meeting." He's impressed. "Yes, Gabe. The Director of Parks. I'm his PA." We're meeting this coming Tuesday. He tells me to wear a red rose in my hair. "No Gabe. Not in my hair. I'll wear my navy suit with a red rose in my lapel, so you'll recognise me." He tells me he'll be carrying a red rose in his mouth. I can't help but laugh.

He's there. Would you believe he's carrying a bouquet of red roses? I'm blown away.

Jeez. He's so thin. I mean he was always tall and lanky, but, when I give him a big hug, I can feel his bones. He's so pale, looks ill. His gums, bleeding. I try not to show my shock at his appearance and bury my face in the gorgeous flowers.

"So, how's life Gabe?"

He looks away, "The company has laid me off."

"Why Gabe? What happened?"

"The gov'ner doesn't need me any more."

I can't believe it. "This is your lucky day Gabe." I fling

my arms round him in excitement then hold him away to look deep into his eyes; "My boss is looking for someone to arrange the firework display at Soldier's field, Roundhay Park this November." To my surprise Gabe doesn't look interested, he's looking away. I need his attention and grip him tightly. He winces in pain and gasps before whispering. "Not sure if I've enough time."

"Course you have Gabe. I'll get you the application forms. He needs someone urgently. It's a huge event, and usually it needs at least 6 months preparation." He just shrugs. I can't help wondering what's wrong with him, but, put his lack of interest down to being a bit depressed having been laid off. Mind you I think he needs to put on a bit of weight. I don't think he's eating properly. Back at work, I tell my boss about Gabriel. He's heard of him through the network. I don't like swearing but what he says is something on the lines of 'Get him here pronto.'

Gabriel arrives loaded with plans and costs, Health & Safety etc., based on one of the jobs he has done recently. I can see the Director is impressed and offers him the contract to start immediately.

It's a short contract, which seems to suit Gabe. He has the freedom and finances to buy all the fireworks, including a special one Gabe has designed and made, which will be set off as the finale to the show. The funds also enable him to recruit his own men to help create and erect the display. Gabe starts work immediately. He has safe premises to store his materials and fireworks. It's where his gang is working at this moment.

Beginning of October Ted, his Chief Ganger, calls me. Gabe has gone downhill. So ill he's in St. Michael's hospice and needs to see me. His diagnosis is Myeloid Leukaemia, a pyro-technician's nemesis, prognosis, not good.

At the Hospice I am shown to his room. He's lying in bed so pale and beautiful. He smiles at me, whispering, "We should have been together Lyn." Weakly holding my hand he nods at his side table. "There's a letter of instruction." He smiles, whispering, "just follow it. To the letter?" I nod, feeling tears forming. His face is radiant.

Ted's waiting for me at the workshop, surrounded by the gang. Gabe's ashes are in a brown cardboard box, bigger than I expected considering the weight Gabe had lost. As I hand Gabe's ashes to Ted I feel tears rolling down my cheeks and question: "Why?" Ted laughs wryly and looks up and round the sky. "He wouldn't, Ted."
   "Why do you think he built his own rocket Lyn?"

The firework display is magnificent. The finale announced over the tannoy, "The wishes of a Master Pyrotechnician, built by Angelo Gabriel, ashes to the stars."

His rocket zooms higher than any other firework at the display. All eyes are on this, his final creation, breathtaking in its magnificence as it reaches its highest point, following the trajectory he planned. It's exploding, releasing thousands of cascading stars. The crowd thinks it's over, but no: three smaller rockets now detonate, zooming further into the darkness of the universe, trailing their coloured sparks of wheeling and jiggling spangled flashing lights that dissolve into rainbows slowly descending to earth. Released at last, Angelo Gabriel's ashes burn in the heavens. Mission achieved; he's gone out with a bang.

Hirsute

Emily Stronach Walker

He was the hairiest baby I'd ever seen. On his head, a thick mop of jet-black hair was slicked down by a white, sticky glue, and across his back and shoulders he had tufts of downy black fuzz. The flurry of midwives scooped him up from Lena's chest and took his measurements, like a prized vegetable. Lena grabbed my hand, exhaling and shaking. She was two people now – part of her existed in this tiny, hairy thing.

"Would mum like to cut the cord?" I was being spoken to. All day I'd been misnamed as mum, or other mum. One doctor even called me dad by accident. I expected this to happen when Lena asked me to be her birth partner, so I quietly mumbled "just a friend" in response. After a while, I stopped correcting the staff.

"No, thank you." I felt lightheaded. I watched the screaming baby relent as midwives chopped the appendage from his belly button, clean off. Snip. A small stump remained protruding from his abdomen with a plastic clothes peg pinned to the end. My gaze then fixated on the puddles of liquid around the end of the bed. The fleshy pouch of the placenta sat dormant, like an embryonic alien primed to leech onto someone's face. Midwives beamed at me, patted me on the shoulder.

When Lena first told me she was pregnant, she was leaning against the sink of a nightclub bathroom, neon paint illuminating her face in the dim light. The club's dank humidity gave her a slight glow, as her teary eyes searched my face for answers. She was scared to be alone. I promised she never would be. I brought her body into mine, embracing her tightly without saying a word. Her hips slowly pressed into me as her arms wrapped tighter across my back, quietly breathing into the crease of my neck. We lingered in those silent moments, until I felt her begin to edge out of my grasp, ready to bring a new future out of the shadows and into focus. I held on tighter, squeezing my eyes shut. *Don't go. Please stay with me.*

"Zoe, come here." Lena whispered to me from the hospital bed, squeezing my hand. I turned to her – her black hair was matted with sweat across her brow, and she smiled at me, her lips quivering. I leaned down towards her and placed my hand on her face, pressing our foreheads together. Then she kissed me for the first time.

*

"Oh wow, what a hairy little man!" A midwife, new to the shift, arrived to conduct her check-ups as Lena slept. She was staring down into the crib. "Mum must have had awful heartburn with you, you little rascal." She talked into the bassinet using the adult-baby voice that made me cringe.

"Why would she have bad heartburn?" I asked. It was true, Lena had moaned about indigestion her entire pregnancy. I always kept a pack of antacids in my bag in case she needed one.

"Bad heartburn in pregnancy is a sign of a hairy baby. It's to do with the hormones." The midwife gently stroked the baby's fur-like hair, jotted something down in her notes then moved on to the adjacent crib. I stared at him, still nameless, unable to connect this new human's arrival with all the ways Lena's body had changed over nine months. How it stretched, then ached, then became captive to his concealed existence.

I must have fallen asleep, because some time later, I woke up in my chair to Lena nudging me, the baby attached to her chest. The white glare of the hospital room blurred my vision, as I became alert to the sound of wriggling, cawing babies. I tried not to grimace at Lena's slightly sour breath or the milk stains on her robe.

"Morning sleepy." She pulled away and wandered to the crib to put the baby down. "I thought I'd better wake you – some of the Mums are coming by for visiting hours." *The Mums.* That was my cue to leave. After packing up my things, I lingered at the end of her bed, the moment too large and our tiredness too palpable to say anything. She hastily kissed me for the second time. I turned out of the room, flushed and dizzy, when I felt something strange and irritable on my tongue. I pulled a long, black hair from my mouth.

*

It had been a week since Lena gave birth and her living room was too cramped for the seven of us. The room had a sweet, creamy muskiness to it, likely from the milk-crusted muslin cloths draped over the sofa. I was penned in place by a fence of Mums, each with a gormless, bug-eyed baby affixed to their chest. I glanced around this semi-circle of floating infants, an air of silent reverence hanging between them, like a congregation of elders ready to begin their ritual. They all looked like copies of the same baby.

Lena was changing her baby, who now went by Elliot, in the bedroom with one of the Mums. We had texted a few times since the birth, still no mention of the kiss. I'd thought about it every day though, replaying the moment again and again, desperate to capture the feeling and keep it. Our foreheads pressed together, the damp heat of her tears and flicker of her eyelashes. Then her lips against mine. Until I remembered the baby, his squirming body fixed into the corner of my memory, clinging to his mother. His *mother.* Lena was a mother. This new identity still seemed untethered to her.

A sharp cackle, and I was back in the living room. I'd tried over the months to learn who was who in the Mum group, but all their names ended with an *a*, so I could never remember. Jessica, Sophia, Laura, Becca, now Lena.

I'd met them all in her prenatal classes, accompanied by their silent husbands. A flurry of questions probed my first visit. How did I know Lena? Was I excited to be a parent? What did I do for a living? Was I married, was Lena my wife? *Who are you and why are you here?* is what they wanted to ask. One of the Mums tried to introduce me to the group of husbands, who added me to their Dad group chat. I deleted it soon after.

"I felt awful after this little one arrived. I couldn't stop going to the toilet." The Mums seemed to speak in a chorus, overlapping each other.

"What a nightmare. Hair loss too, that's another thing they don't tell you about."

"I thought I was going bald!"

"For me it was my tits. They were never the same."

"Mastitis?"

"No, *my tits*. God, I never felt pain like it!"

"All worth it in the end though."

"Absolutely."

"I would do it all again for this one."

"You don't have kids yourself, do you Zoe?" The chorus paused, turned to me.

"No," I replied. "I don't have kids."

"Oh, why not?"

"If you don't mind us asking?"

"I guess whilst you're still studying, you probably can't afford them?"

"I hope we're not prying."

"I just don't want them." I said abruptly, speaking to the floor. A few of the babies stirred – I had upset the council.

"That's okay! You might change your mind, you're still so young!"

"Or you might not, and that's totally okay too." At that moment, Becca/Jessica emerged from the bedroom, holding little Elliot like a trophy. The semicircle of babies parted to accommodate this new member, so I slipped through the gap to find Lena.

The bedroom wall was covered in a large collage of old photos – my eyes always jumped to the ones of me and Lena. The summer school production of *A Midsummer Night's Dream*, our lanky, teenage arms draped around the other, the horse's head that Lena wore to play Bottom balanced on her lap. A photo of our faces after a night-out, the taste of tequila on our tongues, eyeliner smudged down our faces like warpaint. Lena, the day of her twelve-week scan, grinning above the camera lens at me, the enormity of her future on a black-and-white ultrasound image, clutched between her fingers. Lena and I sat staring at the wall of photos, the hum of her breast pump between us.

"God, I used to look great, didn't I," she said. I was unsure which photo she was looking at – it could have been any of them. She instinctively touched her stomach, which was still swollen, although slightly deflated now. Her breasts and hips were rounder, and her skin had broken out into clumps of acne. I avoided staring at a pile of blood-stained knickers and towels in the corner of the room, or the discarded clumps of black hair on the dressing table. I touched her hand resting on the bed.

"You still do." Until she got pregnant, I had never heard Lena talk about her body so much. Sometimes her pregnant body gave her great joy, curves that made her feel womanly, a body that felt purposeful and import-ant. Other times it broke her. She was held hostage to it, plummeting to greater depths of resentment for it, how it leaked and bled and bloated.

"You don't have any indigestion tablets on you, do you?" Lena clutched her chest, awkwardly knocking the breast pump and adjusting it.

"Heartburn still bad?" I reached into my bag for the antacids. She popped out three.

"Oh, every part of me is just malfunctioning!" She forced a laugh, still staring at the photos. Her mouth opened slightly to inhale, then she paused and pouted her lips. "This might sound weird, but could I show you something? It's got me a little worried. And you're always good at reassuring me."

"Sure. What is it?" The gentle hum of the pump continued to whir. Carefully, she removed a large hairclip attached to her head, unleashing a jet-black stream of hair that fell to her hips.

"Your hair's gotten so long!"

"Yes, that too. But there's also this." She pulled the hair behind her ears and tilted closer to my face. I was staring at her ear, and from it, a thick lock of hair grew from inside it. It must have been about five inches long, falling over her ear lobe onto her shoulder, attached to a deeper part of her ear canal I couldn't see. She grabbed the hair and pulled at it. It didn't move.

"That's... not normal, is it?" I stared at it until she swished her hair back round, the lock of ear-hair blending in with the rest of her black mane.

"I don't know what to do about it. I've been cutting it every night this week, but it grows back the same. I'm struggling to get a doctor's appointment, and it's not exactly life-threatening, so I don't think they'd do anything about it. But it's just so *ugly*." I had no idea what to say. Outside, I could hear the Mums shout for Lena – Elliot needed feeding. I stood up to leave and she grabbed my hand. "Zoe, wait. What do you think I should do?" Elliot's hungry cries pierced through the walls, accompanied by shushing and fussing from the chorus of Mums.

"I don't know, I'm sorry." I didn't want to talk about her hair, or her body or her baby, I wanted to return to our kiss, to ask her what it meant and what we should do about it. But she didn't need that right now. "Maybe ask Jessica or one of the others? They'll probably know. Sorry." Lena frowned, moved her hand up to her ear, her cheeks flushed.

"I could – they don't always... I just prefer talking to

you about this kind of thing – " Another Elliot scream burst through the wall and propelled Lena from the bed, brushing past my shoulder and out into the living room. She was met with a resounding cheer.

"Ah Mummy's here!"

"Mummy's here!"

I stayed in her room, staring at the photos of us.

*

My next visit to see Lena wasn't for a while. She sent me a message to say she was feeling unwell and needed some help with Elliot. All her texts had been pictures or updates about the baby, questions that became rhetorical at my ignorance. I didn't know how to change or feed or hold him. I didn't know how to talk about babies, how to interact with them, what they could and couldn't do. And since she showed me her hair, I was so worried that she would break or malfunction in front of me, and I would be powerless to stop it.

I let myself into her apartment, where I could hear her coughing and spluttering from the bedroom. The room was a mess, nappies strewn across the floor, clothes piled into a corner, illuminated by a dancing dog on the TV. The kitchen sink was filled with unwashed dishes and a pot filled with something resembling beef stew.

"Thanks for coming round. I don't feel right." Lena emerged from the bedroom, whimpering baby in hand, and sat on the sofa. She still looked beautiful, though obviously unwell. Her ear-hair was tucked back into a hairgrip, but now I could see thick clumps of fuzz below her chin and down her neck. Even the backs of her hands were clustered with black hair that grew down her arms and elbows.

"It's no problem. How've you been?"

"Awful. I just can't shift this cough, like it's really stuck in there." She paused, rubbing her chest with her free hand, avoiding my eye contact. I made us some tea and sat beside her, watching the dancing dog without speaking. Its cartoonish eyes seemed to roll out of its head, as it walked on its hind legs across a blindingly colourful street. Then Lena broke the silence. "I spoke to the other Mums about my hair." I noticed her lips quivering.

"Oh yeah? What did they say?"

"Not much really. They said it's probably just my hormones resettling, and it'll fall out on its own."

"I guess that makes sense." Elliot wriggled in her arms, restless, agitated. "If there's anything you need me to help with – " Lena started coughing again, dry and raspy at first. She handed me the baby who squirmed uneasily in my arms. His abnormal mop of fuzzy, black hair bristled against my chin as he wriggled. Her coughing then descended into a dense, mucus-coated hacking. Lena grabbed her chest, fumbling with the other hand to steady herself. Elliot started crying.

I reached for a muslin cloth and dangled it in front of his face, attempting to distract him. Then Lena started gagging. Her whole body shuddered and convulsed, her chest heaved in a laboured rhythm, like something was lodged, edging itself out. Her black hair, neatly set by the hairgrip, unravelled down her back, as the hair from inside her ears also fell loose down her shoulders.

Lena fell to the floor, back hunched and retching. She took shallow, pained breaths between convulsions, as if breathing was now secondary to the force overcoming her. Pushing something up. And out.

Eventually, she reached her hand into her mouth and clawed at her tongue, then deeper to the back of her throat. She grabbed something and pulled. Clasped between her fingers, stringy with saliva, was a clump of black hair. She pulled again, so the thick knot unravelled out of her mouth and over her chin.

Neither of us spoke at first. Her heavy spasms stopped, although tremors still rippled through her body. She looked up at me, the thick lock of hair hanging down towards her neck. Her hand, still shaking, reached up to touch it, and gently gave it a tug. It didn't move.

"Open your mouth wide." My voice came out hoarse. She seemed almost infantile, obligingly opening her mouth like she was going to show me a missing tooth. I peered in. The hair stretched to the back of her tongue, past her tonsils and down her gullet. I grimaced. She scurried away to look at herself in the mirror. My arms ached from carrying Elliot. The dog on TV was suddenly eclipsed by a black, pop-up message across the screen. *Are you still there?* it asked.

"What should I do?" Lena had her back to me, facing the mirror. She sounded as if she was trying to chew something, and her words came out muffled and choked. "Zoe, tell me what to do." I wanted to run or phone for help, but the desperation on her face halted me, reminded me what she meant to me. I couldn't leave her.

*

We tried cutting the hair at first. Propped up on the bed, we balanced a light over her mouth as she pressed her tongue into the fleshy cavern below it, so I could see the hair stretch down her throat. It had a moist consistency and had begun to curl at the end, forming a ringlet. My toes curled every time I brought the scissors to her mouth, so scared I would accidentally cut her gum. Snip. The hair dropped into a fallen ponytail and Lena scooped it away into the bin. The following morning, the hair had grown back thicker and longer. In a panic, she suggested bleaching it or throwing chemicals onto it, an idea I quickly dismissed.

As the days blurred into weeks, it became clear that her hair needed its own kind of treatment. It turned oily and the ends frayed. She couldn't bear the taste of shampoo, so we concocted a cleanser from eggs and lemon juice to wash it. I bought her a special brush that would help her unknot it. I even started trimming it to remove the split ends. We tolerated its presence – its maintenance became habitual to us.

Lena went to see her doctor, who was less surprised and more curious. He told her he'd seen a lot of strange post-partum symptoms in his time. As long as she wasn't in pain, there was nothing he could do.

"What the hell does he know?" I was furiously assembling some of Elliot's wooden blocks as Lena relayed the doctor's words. "He doesn't see how much this *bothers* you. Shall we go back together? I can be there for moral support if you'd like." Lena chuckled.

"I like how defensive you are." She suggested we try ways to disguise the hair. We experimented with hiding it in scarves and long baggy hats, or styling her head-hair in a way that would allow the mouth-hair to blend in. After a while, she practised positioning it to sit neatly down the cavern of her mouth and emerge from the corner of her lips. It required some training, but it meant she could speak normally without chewing on it.

Once we cracked that, she started venturing out of the house more, tackling the supermarket and post office by herself. I even persuaded her to start going to a local baby group with the Mums. Thankfully, she didn't ask me to join. Elliot was beginning to move further away from an anonymous newborn, turning into a small human with a personality. He liked red objects. He hated his nappy being changed. He laughed when someone sneezed. He even felt quite warm and comforting in my arms and didn't seem too bothered if I wasn't holding him right.

"He loves my new hair, you know." Lena said to me one day. Elliot, now a giggly, grabby four-month-old, was lying on his baby mat, Lena and I sat beside him. The hair from her mouth, a thick shock of ebony emerging from the corner of her lips, had been tied into a loose plait that fell over her breasts and hips. Elliot was tugging it gently.

"I like how happy it makes him." She held the end of the plait and tickled it on Elliot's nose, laughing and smiling at his fascination with the braid. He was less mysterious to me than when he was born, thankfully less bloody too, but just as fear-inducing. I couldn't begin to quantify everything he had done, how much Lena had changed for him.

She looked up at me and held my gaze, her eyes wide and beautiful. I imagined my hips pressed into hers, running my fingers down her neck and the small of her back, wanting to envelope her into my arms and pick up where we had left off in the hospital room. There would be time for all of that. I shuffled closer to her and nestled into her shoulder, watching Elliot play with her hair.

Silent Cure

Hannah Walton-Hughes

"You are so close, Brenda." I whisper. "Just think!"

But she carries on staring at the table of test tubes, PH strips and disposable gloves, forehead scrunched up in concentration. After a few more seconds of this, she appears to crumple. Her face collapses into itself like a piece of old parchment, and she falls forwards onto the table, her arms coming forward to create a pillow for her head.

I wrap my arms around her shoulders, kissing the top of her head; that always used to comfort her. But not today. How could it? How could *I*?

There is a reason why everyone refers to Cancer as the Big C. Big Cliff. Big Climb. Big Chase. Big Crap. And many other words that I am too polite to say.

It was my own Cancer that prompted my beautiful daughter, Brenda, to dedicate her life to finding a cure. Brenda and the rest of the world. But she has somehow convinced herself that *she* will be the one to find it, having just graduated from medical school, the top of her class. I wasn't about to question her, but I do wish she wouldn't always get her hopes up quite so much. It would make things much easier.

I was young when I had Brenda; it wasn't exactly planned. I wouldn't have changed it for the world, but I do wonder if some of that early stress was part of what made me more vulnerable to...

Anyway, thank God I had her then, because if I had waited until later, I might never have had the chance to have a child.

I remember when the doctor first handed her to me, after nearly fourteen hours of excruciating labour. The feeling of terror that initially filled me. And then the intense feeling of calm that followed when I looked down at her little face and thought – this is what I have been waiting for my whole life. My sole purpose on Earth was always to raise this gorgeous little angel.

Since Cancer, everything looks different to me. It is as if someone has gone over the world with a well-defined marker. I can see life clearly, and with less bias than before. Not without any bias, mind you, I am still human! Rather, I notice things I didn't before, pick up on solutions to problems that were simply too complicated for me to comprehend in my pre-Cancer state.

One of these solutions, I believe, is nothing less than the ultimate cure for Cancer. The key to abolishing the Big C.

In order to achieve validation, I decide to consult my best friend, Margaret. We met each other during our second round of chemo, and bonded over our intense dislike of one particular nurse, who spoke to us like we were babies, and always stunk of tobacco. Margaret had been on board with some of the top Cancer researches in the world, so she really knows all experiments undertaken. It was almost the Earth's cruel sense of humour; she had spent her life devoted to defeating the monster in order to save everyone else, and yet she couldn't escape it when it came after her.

"Cathy!" Margaret answers in her business-like voice. "What can I do for you?"

"I think I've got it, Margo."

"Sorry, you think you've got what?"

"The solution to all our problems."

*

The cup of coffee rests in my fist, burning my skin, but I hardly even notice. Pain has been minimised for me. Margaret doesn't drink coffee – I don't know how she focuses on the multitude of tasks she is supposed to complete on a daily basis without it, but there we go. The bitter taste swirls around my mouth, and warms me to the very bone, emanating the familiar caffeine rush. Once I have finished telling Margaret everything, she is silent, but when she turns to me, her eyes are gleaming with a newfound hope.

"Well, you've done it." she says quietly.

"Pardon?"

"You've done it, darling! You've cracked it!"

And we throw our arms around each other, and jump up and down like little girls at a birthday party.

*

When I get home that evening, neither my husband nor my daughter are anywhere to be seen. Sometimes I open the door so quietly that they don't even realise I am in the room until I am right next to them. Then they jump, and I get annoyed, and they get annoyed, and then we all end up laughing about it, and agreeing that I should wear a bell or something round my neck to announce my arrival.

Today though, I find my husband slumped at the kitchen table, a half empty bottle of beer at his side. It is this sight that makes me feel as though a dagger has been plunged into my heart. My strong, reliable, ever-cheerful husband, Raymond, showing his pain. I realise that this has been harder for him than for anyone else. Not only has he had to mask his own pain from me, but he has tried to put on the pretence of hope for Brenda.

When I first told them both about my diagnosis, Brenda immediately burst into tears and started screaming about how unfair it all was, leaving the room with a slam of the door. But Raymond took a deep breath, swallowed, and reached for my hand. And he said one single sentence. Just one sentence.

"We are going to beat this my darling."

That was all he needed to say. *We* will beat this. Because we are a team. We always have been.

Most of the time, when there is an accidental pregnancy

and people get married shortly after, it is out of a feeling of obligation. Not with us. We both knew the marriage would have happened eventually.

I gently go to remove the can of beer from the table, but then think better of it. If that is what Raymond needs to make himself feel better, than who am I to take that away, especially since I am the one who has put him in hell? So instead I do the only thing I can do. I wrap my arms around him. He doesn't respond. All that happens is a small tear-drop runs down his nose and drops onto the table.

*

I set off bright and early the next morning; Brenda has obviously slept at her office again. She always does that when she thinks she is close to a breakthrough. I hope she won't be disappointed or offended that I am the one to have found that breakthrough. Part of the reason I hadn't told her that I was developing my own ideas about the cure was because I was hoping, for the sake of her pride, that she would get there first. Brenda is generally very highly strung, and does not always react in the way one would expect. Deep down, she will be happy that I have found a solution, but she suffers from an inferiority complex that means she will come out with something cutting like, "Oh, so you're the Cancer expert now, are you?" Well, yes Brenda, I am.

In many ways, she is still just a teenager.

Brenda is not at the lab. I know my daughter like the back of my hand, so I follow the path of her favourite walk, through the trees and over the hills and fields that are so well hidden by the stone grey research laboratory that she spends too much time in. The breeze is a little too much for me today, and I wrap my shawl more tightly around myself.

The churchyard really isn't far. I know I will find her in the same spot she always is. By the gravestone that is in the direct shadow of the church spire. She knew that the person whom the headstone belonged to preferred the shade to the sun. She knew that person like the back of her hand.

Sometimes she sits here and talks to the headstone. Sometimes her shoulders shake with repressed sobs. Today, she just sits solemnly, staring at the name so intently that you would think a television set was placed there.

I move towards her with an eagerness that I haven't felt since the Cancer. I bend so that my mouth is as close as possible to her ear, and whisper the cure I have discovered. I wait for her reaction. None. I try again, my frustration growing.

That is when it starts happening. I feel a tingling sensation spreading through my body, and a swooping feeling, as though a vacuum is been coursed through me.

No! I haven't had enough time. Forget the cure. I've not had enough time to tell her everything she needs to know. To tell her that she will be ok ... even without me.

I try one more time, but it is no good. The sky is opening up, and I am blending into the clouds. I can see my mother reaching her hand out to me, smiling. *It's time, Cathy*, are the words that her lips form.

Then I see Margaret, standing a few feet from Brenda, head bowed. For a second, I wish that it was her turn to leave, not mine. After all, she is the same as me. Her remaining presence here on Earth is also limited by the Big C's best friend – Death. But then I realise she can finish what I've started. She can try to communicate with my baby girl, and, just perhaps, bring to the world the cure that everyone needs.

Because, God knows, my family could have done with a spirit who has a new perspective on everything, especially Cancer.

I love you baby.

Those are the last words that escape my parched mouth, before my mother embraces me. I strain my neck round and lock eyes with Margaret.

Look after her.

I will.

Just for a second, the girl kneeling by my grave looks up, as if she hears something. *Mum?*

That is the last thing I hear before I and the cure are soaked into the heavenly abyss.

Anatomy

Kate Vine

We first met in a queue, on a glass-like night.

He commented that it was too hot for May – *where had it come from?* he asked, *this heat?*

I don't remember how I replied, which words I used.

*

I wait for you. Among the people and pints and packets of crisps –

I wait.

I'm patient, I know you'll come. That look in your eyes, piercing the crowd to reach me, unscathed. But I don't know about her

yet.

*

It's phrases I remember. He said –

Where is home?

I looked at him over a glass of wine that stung my tongue and told him I'd never had a real home. But I'd like one, I said, a place where uncertainty finally stopped tapping between my shoulders. He was from Glasgow where his mother lived, aunts lived, cousins lived, friends from since he was born lived. I could see it in the way he held himself, safe in the knowledge then when he fell, they would catch him.

He said –

I'm not sure my happiness is within my control.

I told him how some days I felt darkness no matter how strong the sunlight; how others were dreary and yet I revelled in them. But that was more like mood than contentment, he said. He envied those who were content in the smallness of things.

He said –

I want to see you tomorrow.

It wasn't a question. I couldn't imagine why we'd spend tomorrow doing anything other than what we were doing at that moment: unpeeling each other to see if what lay beneath tasted as good as it looked.

*

You don't lie but you don't tell me
  either.
  I find her on the screen of my phone, images that move at the touch of my fingers. I slid through image
  after image
  after
  The pain is not that she is yours, that you are hers, it's the
  Barcelona sand between rough toes
  moving boxes and windows without curtains
  pub garden celebrating
  one
  two
  three
  four
  five years that you've been in her life
  and not mine.

*

I joined him the next day to walk along the canal. He could tell that I knew, that I'd studied their life, documented in filtered photographs. He walked a few steps ahead and said,

We can be friends, though – right?

But it wasn't friendship I sought. I wanted more than my

life had thus far given me.

We talked but I felt sharpened into an unbearable point; when his lips moved, I tasted the canal water beside us. He told me that his father died when he was young, and it confused him – not knowing such a large part of himself.

My mum stares at me sometimes. It's like she's searching for him.

For hours, we walked past streets and pubs and old factories. The evening brought a cold wind. Without thinking, I reached for his hand and, when that felt good, I reached for the other. He looked at the myriad of fingers, tangled together like weeds, and sighed.

*

We take the coach out of town so that we're not
seen.
I struggle with my seatbelt and you don't think to help.
You are nervous.
I lean into your warm arm and feel the tension lessen as we move from city into countryside. We talk and you laugh, and I wonder how different you'd look if unhindered by guilt. But is anyone ever
unhindered?
We shouldn't, you say
you shouldn't, they say
But no one tells me how to do it, to give up the one person who looks at me and
sees.

*

We sat on stools in a café, a round table between us. He told me he couldn't see me anymore if we were going to be –
this.
I said we couldn't be anything else.

A week later he called, waking me in the night, but dis-connecting when I answered. Then a message –
I don't know what to do.
He knocked on my door. I expected him to look sad, but his face was alive. He kissed me with his whole body, in my hallway, while the rest of the street slept on.

*

With my finger, I trace the tattoos on your skin I'd mistak-en for chest hair at first. You aren't bald on the chest, but it's not what I expected. I'd imagined a you
that doesn't exist.
We can't lie together often, though it's my favourite thing: to put my head on your stomach and listen to your digestion. Fluid moving round your insides, just as I would, if I was
small enough.

*

He told me the strangest part was walking from my place back to his, like travelling from one self to another. I didn't tell him how I saw his mind return to her even when he was inside me, how the two selves were not only together, they were fighting, wrestling, groaning.
I let him believe what he needed to keep coming back.

*

She
isn't as beautiful as I first thought. In most pictures, her face holds the same pose, tilted to the same angle, the same teeth exposed. These are easier to
ignore
than the ones where she's looking at you.
At first, I feel guilt; next, I feel pity. But then it contorts,

becomes something like obsession.

I stare at her every day, every night.

I dissect her, piece by piece, to find the part that made you love her.

*

I bought a ticket to see him read at the bookshop, and a new shirt to wear that night too. I would outshine her, I decided. I would hear his new poetry, look into the words and see, for the first time, myself reflected back.

I arrived early, the crowd brightly coloured in headscarves, jewellery and denim. Stood at the front, he seemed proud and satisfied. But then I saw her by his side in a black polo neck, long hair hanging loose and tucked behind her ear. She laughed and pulled her handbag higher up her shoulder like the woman I wasn't, that I knew I'd never be.

Until then, I thought I knew exactly what I had chosen. But I watched them both, so very much
   together
   and saw how little I'd understood.

*

You're not making sense.
   I'm trying!
   Tears through words, coughing on salt water
   you stand
   without clothes
   and try to make things better. Or, at least, to explain that with her you have
   memories and plans and
   another family who count you as their own.
   It's too complex a knot to untie.
   But people do, I say. *They meet someone else. They move on.*

You put a hand to my jaw, tilt my gaze to meet yours,
tears sliding beneath your fingerprints –
Listen to me – no, listen!
But I can't; you won't say what I need to hear, and I am
tired – I am so tired. I want you more than I knew it was
possible
   to want.

*

He wouldn't give me what I needed, so he gave me the
rest.
   Sex in my bed
   my kitchen
   my garden
   my car
   even his bed – their bed – when I insisted.
   He kept his body close to mine: he saw what I couldn't,
that I'd begun to slip away.
   He held me down, trapped my wrists above my head.
   Lie still.

*

She
   leaves you
   before I have the strength to. She has felt you split in two
and she only wanted you
   whole.
   I hear that she's moved out, that she's staying with her
parents, back in Scotland, where the pair of you met
   and fell in love.
   You're not the same without her. You won't look me in
the eye, you flinch at my touch. In one final way, she has
triumphed.
   Though could any of us really win
   this game?

There was no point I could press my finger against and say
there it is, that's it. He was here until
he wasn't.
The pain was blatant and unyielding. I stared at the
screen, watching him come on and offline, typing messages I never sent. I didn't wash my sheets, instead wrapping
them round my body, breathing in his skin cells, his smell.
She
repeated on me like a sickening flavour. I'd taken from
her the very things I wanted most, dismantling her life
without thinking of how she would continue after, surrounded by broken parts.
He and I didn't take only from each other.
But I couldn't regret. Something had flown in with the
May heat, a need I'd never acknowledged, a longing I
couldn't satiate. I drank him in, every inch, only to empty
the glass before my thirst was quenched.
No, I didn't regret that he came.
But I didn't regret that he was gone
either.

I think of you
sometimes
when I queue for the bus, or when the sky is tinged pink
by the sunshine to come.
I see your book in shop windows, hear your voice on the
radio, read your name and my breath –
stops.
When you left, I searched inside myself; I dug in my nails
and scratched
and scraped
and pulled
until I tore it free – the part you had made.

And yet, sometimes
still
I feel you there, nonetheless. I think of you and I am heavy.
I am heavy.

Food Chain

Anna Chilvers

When the child was confined to bed, Valeria started watching the trains. They'd been passing through the valley the whole time, but she hadn't been paying attention, they were just the background noise to her nightmare. The sickness, the fevers, the sudden rushes to the bathroom in the night which didn't always get there in time. She hated it with all her being. She hadn't signed up to be a nurse, she didn't want to spend her days mopping up the bodily secretions of another person.

The worst part was the child's crying, the child's fear. Valeria knew she should be offering comfort and reassurance. She could picture it in her mind. She could see her arm around the child's body, feel the thin hot shoulder bones pressing the flesh of her upper arm. She could hear her own voice *it will be OK, we'll find what you need, someone will have blood for you.* She could feel the pressure against her right breast as she drew the child nearer in a small hug, and smelled his unwashed hair.

She drew back out of the hallucination. A train had drawn into the station. It was 6.33am and this was the third train of the day. From her kitchen window overlooking the tracks she watched the carriages rolling by as the brakes squealed and the train pulled alongside the platform. None of the passengers were sitting close to each other. There were only one or two in each carriage, three in the last. Nine passengers on the whole train, plus the driver.

The child's legs had given way last night. She'd had to carry him to the bedroom. Today she would see if she could find some nappies. He wouldn't like it, but what else could she do? He couldn't walk to the bathroom anymore, and he couldn't just piss the bed.

It was so long now since he'd fed that there wasn't much except piss. You could get pull-up nappies, like pants. She'd seen them on the television when she was sitting up with him when the fever was worst. She'd go when the sun was highest. She'd make sure he drank water before he fell sleep for the day. She'd try to say something reassuring to him.

The 6.55 train had fifteen passengers. But these morning trains weren't going to be of any use to her.

In the supermarket everything was too bright and too yellow. She was glad of her sunglasses and the mask which filtered the shining air. She'd covered herself completely. No one would think it was strange, they'd just think she was more paranoid than most. She hadn't got sick herself yet, but that would come eventually if her hunger continued. She walked past the meat counter and the smell of animal blood made her gag. Her empty stomach gurgled with acid as she averted her gaze from glistening liver, shining blue entrails, the split gore of an open stomach, the spill of bile – she shook herself. The meat was packaged in plastic parcels, each packed with a square of gauze to absorb the blood. There were no unsightly secretions.

The dry dust of bread from the bakery was blocking her airways and she hurried on. She found nappies. The signs advised that customers were limited to three purchases of each item, so she bought three packs of the largest size. She hoped they would fit the child. He was no infant, but his hips were thin and bony, she had seen toddlers in the streets who had more flesh on them, more blood in their plump bodies.

There was a difficult moment near the check out. Valeria had chosen self-service to avoid any polite chitchat with the check-out operator. There were squares marked out on the floor with tape, and it seemed that some people were quicker to pick up on the new rules than others. She was scanning the barcode on the nappies when she smelled blood, right there beside her, warm and pulsing through veins no more than a foot away. She wasn't in the same state of starvation as the child, but it had been a long time since she fed. It took muscular strength to control the urge to turn and snap.

She held herself still, then turned her head to see a man holding two four-packs of beer.

"Please could you step back a little."

"Sorry love."

He shuffled away from her and she smelled the alcohol, lifting from the pores of his skin, mingling with his breath. She couldn't judge anyone's habits. Drinking beer in the morning might be the best response to this situation.

The child was sleeping soundly when she returned. Valeria managed to manoeuvre his body and slip on one of the pull-up nappies. She wiped a hand across his brow, and imagined it was a gesture of affection. Perhaps once someone did love this child. Now the two of them were in it together.

She returned to the kitchen and drank water to cool her hunger. She watched the trains and made notes of the times they went past, the number of passengers on each. People waited on the bone-white concrete of the platform. Each train arrived, then left a few minutes later leaving the platform wiped clean. Nobody ever seemed to get off. She knew this couldn't be true, that it was a trick of the light or the time of day. The sun glanced off the metal sides of the trains. She had no reason to go out again today. The breeze moved the new leaves on the trees that lined the tracks.

In winter, the view from this kitchen window was of straight tracks, bare branches, brown lines at angles from each other. Now it had become bucolic, picturesque, the lines hidden by a profusion of life and sap, even blossom. If only leaves had something more potent than chlorophyll running through them, there would be no danger of starvation.

At dusk she opened her window and scattered a few sunflower seeds, then stood to the side and waited. It took a while. Perhaps the birds were passing on messages to each other, and knew that this sill was best avoided, however tasty the treats. But after a while a small brown bird landed and began to peck at the seeds. It wasn't a sparrow, she recognised sparrows. This was slightly larger, duller in colour. She suspected it was female – in the bird world it's the males that have the shine and the colour. Valeria watched the sharp jerky movements, the slight convulsion of the gullet, the eyes bright as jet. If she waited any longer it would fly off.

Her movement was quicker than the bird's; it didn't have time to react. Her arm reached, snatched, twisted – the bird was dead before it even knew it had been caught. In the kitchen she took a glass from the cupboard with her left hand, held the bird over it and squeezed. She had a grip of iron. Various people had told her this over the years. Her grip of iron closed around the bird, squeezing out the life blood until all she was holding was a mass of feather, bone and skin. She'd got quite efficient at this, but there still wasn't much in the glass. It would keep the child alive for another night, but it couldn't continue much longer. Bird blood was thin; it didn't have the right proteins. Every night the child was weaker.

Later, when she held the glass to his lips, he cried. He hadn't even noticed he was wearing a nappy. His eyes were covered with a pink film.

It would have to be tomorrow.

The night was taken up with the child, holding him, rocking him, stroking his head when the pain got too much for him to bear. His cries set off a jangling between her ears which she recognised as fury. She wanted him to stop. She wanted to place her iron grip against his mouth to shut off the sound, she wanted to crush him like the bird so she didn't have to care for him anymore. She held him against her breast and felt his feverish heat pass through her skin. Eventually, as dawn approached, he calmed. She changed the nappy, she covered him with a sheet, she wondered how it would feel to kiss his hot cheek, or the wet lashes which flickered against them.

The problem was she couldn't take the child on the train, no one would accept that was reasonable. If he was so ill he needed hospital, then she should call an ambulance – that's what they would think. She'd be challenged. Which meant she had to get him on unseen. He had to be hidden. He was bird-thin, his ribs and cheekbones jagged, but he was not a baby. She guessed his age, in human terms, to be seven or eight. She could, in theory, fold him into a suitcase or large bag. But that wouldn't work either – why would she be travelling with luggage? The only permissible reason to take the train was to get to work, and then only if your work was essential, unavoidable. She didn't want to draw attention to herself.

The only way was to attach the child to her own body. She wasn't emaciated like him, but she was slender. If she could attach him to her body, and cover them both up, she might pass as a much larger person.

She checked through the cupboards in the house. There were lots of clothes left by previous occupants, and their victims. When people left they usually only took the clothes they were standing up in. Travel light – it was the best way to move through the world. There were dresses, jackets, jeans, shirts. Some of them bloodstained.

At the back of the wardrobe in the smallest room was a large green military-type coat. She put it on and looked in the mirror on the back of the door. It swamped her. She'd need to build up her shoulders to fill it out. She could use some of the other clothes to do that – fashion some shoulder pads out of knitted jumpers. She'd cover her face, no one would suspect. Covering up was the norm.

She found scarves and stocking in a drawer and spent

the afternoon tying them together. She needed to bind the child to herself securely, but she didn't want to bruise his skin. And when the time was right, she'd need to let him loose. He'd have to feed for himself.

She woke him at sunset. She'd not woken him for weeks, preferring to let him sleep as long as possible, knowing that when he woke, he'd present her with his hunger. She thought of baby birds in the nest with their open beaks, waiting for the mother to return, the mother she'd crushed in her hand last night. Valeria wasn't doing any better. She might be there with the child, but she hadn't been able to provide.

He was weaker than ever. She placed an arm behind his shoulder and pushed him upright. He looked at her with clouded eyes. His lips were dried and sealed together. She licked her finger and ran it along his lower lip, separating it from the top.

"We're going out," she said.

She saw a flicker of hope spark for a moment, but even that took too much energy from him.

Strapping him to her was difficult. She asked him to cling to her, just for a moment, whilst she arranged the ties. He tried, but she felt him slipping and had to support him with one hand whilst she strapped him into place with the other. By the time she'd done, he'd gone limp, giving her the whole of his body weight. She thought he'd gone back to sleep, but when she looked in the mirror she saw his eyes were open. She put the shoulder pads in place, shrugged on the coat and buttoned it up. She wrapped her head in scarves and looked in the mirror. If you looked closely you might think her misshapen, oddly formed. But no one would be looking closely. That was the point. That was the problem. There was no one about.

She was the only one waiting on the platform. She'd decided to go for the seven minutes past ten. She wanted darkness and shadows to stand in whilst she waited, but she didn't want to risk an empty train. She'd seen some, as midnight approached, passing through the valley with empty coaches, only the driver breathing in the whole rattling tube. She needed there to be a handful of passengers.

When it arrived she sighed with relief. The first carriage in, nearest the driver, had three passengers. Two were sitting together at a table, and one at the other end. The next carriage was empty, and the third had just one passenger. She stepped into the middle carriage.

There were two stops before they reached the tunnel – four miles long and deep beneath the hills. The train took six minutes to go through it before emerging in another county. There was no phone signal in the tunnel, and it was long enough for the child to drink his fill.

The train rattled through the valley. Valeria wished she could see out. Darkness hadn't completely fallen and she would have like to see the hills, black against the almost-black of the sky, the stars appearing above the solidity of moorland. But the lights inside the train only allowed for glaring reflections. She felt the child stir against her chest. At least he was still alive.

At the next station one extra woman got into the front carriage, and at the station after that no one got on or off. Valeria thought about the person sitting alone in the third carriage. She could almost hear the blood pumping around their body, she could smell iron and salt.

As the train started to move, so did she.

She felt the child pushing against her. From somewhere his skinny limbs had found strength and he was desperate to get free.

"Shh," she whispered. "Soon."

She opened the door between the carriages and stepped over the join just as they entered the tunnel. A narrow corridor took them past the toilet. The door was open, and a smell of disinfectant and urine wafted out, but was totally overpowered by the smell of fresh blood pumping around a body. She couldn't hold on to the child anymore. His frantic struggles broke the bonds and he leapt from her arms, raced down the carriage and launched at the passenger, sinking his teeth into their jugular vein.

It was too fast for there to be any resistance. The child's hunger was so voracious that it only took seconds for the man to have lost a disabling amount of blood. He slumped against the window as the child fed from his neck.

Valeria watched. The man was in his forties, healthy, wearing high visibility clothing, probably on his way to work, or on his way home. His face was florid and his hair black. He was a good size, there would be more than enough blood for them both. She could see the child's body changing as he drank. He filled out before her eyes. The slack skin became taut, the hollow limbs expanded until they were plump and firm, his colour changed from faded parchment to rosy pink. His cheeks moved in and out as he sucked, and his throat made a rhythmic swallowing sound. A trickle of blood dribbled from the corner of his mouth. Valeria wiped it off with a finger and licked it. It was delicious. The man let out a sigh between closed lips.

Eventually the child was sated, and detached from the man's neck. He was unrecognisable from the bag of bones she'd strapped to herself earlier. He was a golden haired child with a cheeky glint in his blue eyes, flushed as though from exercise. His smile was infectious and she found herself chucking him under the chin. No wonder she'd agreed to take him under her wing – he was utterly delightful.

"You must feed now," he said to her.

There was no time to waste. She put her mouth to the wound in the man's neck and drank. She'd almost forgotten that feeling of life flooding in, it had been so long. She shouldn't drain the man; that would bring complications she didn't want to deal with. But it was difficult. She felt the child tugging at her coat.

"Enough!"

She lifted her head and felt the wet blood on her face. The

man had very little left, and he wouldn't live. She hadn't really thought beyond this point. She wouldn't normally leave a body in the open. She tried, as far as possible, never to leave a body. In normal times there were enough people about that she could take a little here and a little there, and the donors barely remembered. They might feel some soreness on the neck, a little light-headedness which quickly dissipated with hot tea or chocolate.

There was nothing to be done though. They would get off at the next station. There was no need to wait for the train home. Now they had strength in their bodies they could run back across the moors.

The man's body slid off the seat and under the table as the train came out of the tunnel.

The light was blinding. Valeria shielded her eyes with her arm, and the child hid in the folds of her coat. The train was stopping too soon. The station wasn't for a while after the tunnel, but the doors were opening. Someone blew a whistle, and there was shouting.

"Everybody off, everybody off." A man in uniform climbed into the carriage. "Out you get, move along, move along."

He didn't notice the body under the table, but hurried Valeria and the child off the train and onto a platform. Another uniformed man had a clipboard. "There should be five on this one," he said to the first man.

The passengers from the front carriage were being pushed in their direction, blinking in the glare of the spotlights. The couple and the man who'd been on already, and the woman who got on at the next stop, all huddled in a group with Valeria and the child.

"Looks like we've got a stowaway," said the man with the board. "There's six here."

"This one has its young with it. There aren't meant to be any immature specimens, only adults."

"I'll take it with me," said the first man. "The boss will tell me what to do with it."

He grabbed hold of the child before Valeria realised what was happening, but she wasn't worried. No man was a match for the child when he had just fed. She waited for the surprise on the officer's face, the cracking of bones.

It didn't come. The man held the struggling child firmly under one arm as he walked away across the station. The boy's blue eyes darted frantically.

"Come on the rest of you," called the man with the board. "We haven't all day. There are three more shipments to come in before the next load is full. Move on, move on."

The small group of five were herded along the platform, too bewildered to look at each other. The high roof of the station was domed and clustered with spotlights glaring white light. The exit doors were wide open and the light from them was even brighter. Valeria thought she heard a high pitched squeal as she and the others were pushed through them into nothing.

Contributor Biographies

A librarian by day, LMA Bauman-Milner is steeped in words until her fingers get wrinkly. Outside of the library, she battles demons, both real and imagined, with whatever tools are close at hand.

John Biglands' stories tend to have a speculative edge and focus on themes of childhood, nature and loss. If you've read a story of his then he would like to thank you. It means the world to him.

Lucy Brighton is a Barnsley-based writer. She teaches and writes and has ridiculous conversations with her naughty dog, Loki. She has been published in: *Writers Forum*; *Journeys: A Space for Words*; Henshaw Press' second anthology; *Shooter* and various places online and on the radio.

Kate Burke is a writer of fiction. She is from Chorley, Lancashire and lives in Manchester. She has written for stage, screen, and more recently, short story anthologies.

Glenis Burgess started writing about 12 years ago. She tends to write for her own benefit, relishing structuring a piece of work to both give readers enough to follow the story, but not enough to tell them everything.

Anna Chilvers is the author of three novels: *East Coast Road*, *Falling Through Clouds*, and *Tainted Love*, all published by Bluemoose Books. Her book of short stories, *Legging It*, was published by Pennine Press in 2012. She is interested in the links between writing and walking and the landscape, and in 2015 received a grant from the Arts Council to walk the five hundred miles from St Abbs in Scotland to Ely in Cambridgeshire as research for a novel.

Sarah Davy is a writer, facilitator and mentor based in rural Northumberland. Her short fiction is published online and in print, and she won the Finchale Award for Short Fiction at the 2023 Northern Writers Awards.

Monica Dickson writes short fiction. Her stories have appeared online, on air and in print journals and anthologies. She has long and shortlisted for various competitions and won the 2019 NoShoSto Flash Fiction Slam. She is a 2021 Academy graduate.

Lydia Gill is a teacher, living and working with adults with learning disabilities in the Esk Valley Camphill Community. Her short stories have been published online, in print and most recently in Salt's anthology of *Best British Short Stories 2023*.

C S Mee grew up in Birkenhead and now lives in Durham, after years studying literature and languages in the UK and elsewhere. She is writing a collection of short stories inspired by the extraordinary world of babies and children.

S K Perry is a writer, lecturer and community organiser living in Chapeltown, Leeds. Sarah's novel *Let Me Be Like Water* was published by Melville House. She is currently on parental leave.

Vicky K Pointing's short stories and flash fiction have been published by Cossmass Infinities, Postcard Shorts, 101 Words, and Expanded Horizons. She completed an MA in Creative Writing in 2016 and won a place in the 2022 Northern Short Story Academy.

Miranda Roszkowski hails from Swansea and lives in Halifax, West Yorkshire. She writes fiction and plays and is the creator/editor of *100 Voices*, a collection of stories of achievement by women from across the UK, published by Unbound in 2022. Her writing has been published in literary magazines and performed by the National Theatre Wales and is often focused on women's voices and around the theme of belonging, which is important when you have a surname as long as hers. Above all, she is passionate about great stories and who gets to tell them.

Rob Schofield is a fiction writer whose first novel won a Northern Writers Debut Fiction award. His short stories have been published online and in journals and have been long and shortlisted for prizes including the Manchester Fiction Prize.

Lyn Towers' three loves in her life are her dog, allotment and Jim her husband, not necessarily in that order. She writes short stories and poetry, some have been published locally and nationally. She is seeking publication for her novel.

Emily Stronach Walker is a writer from York who has been published in Ellipsis Zine and the York Literary Review. She has recently completed an MA in Creative Writing and loves writing about weird, transforming bodies in her fiction.

Hannah Walton-Hughes is a creative writer from York. She has submitted her short stories to various competitions, receiving a number of awards. Hannah is in the process of completing her first novel, a psychological thriller entitled *The Murder Inside Me*.

Kate Vine has an MA in Creative Writing from UEA and her short fiction has been shortlisted for the Bath Short Story Award and published by Lunate, Retreat West and Dear Damsels among others. She's represented by Charlotte Seymour at Johnson & Alcock.